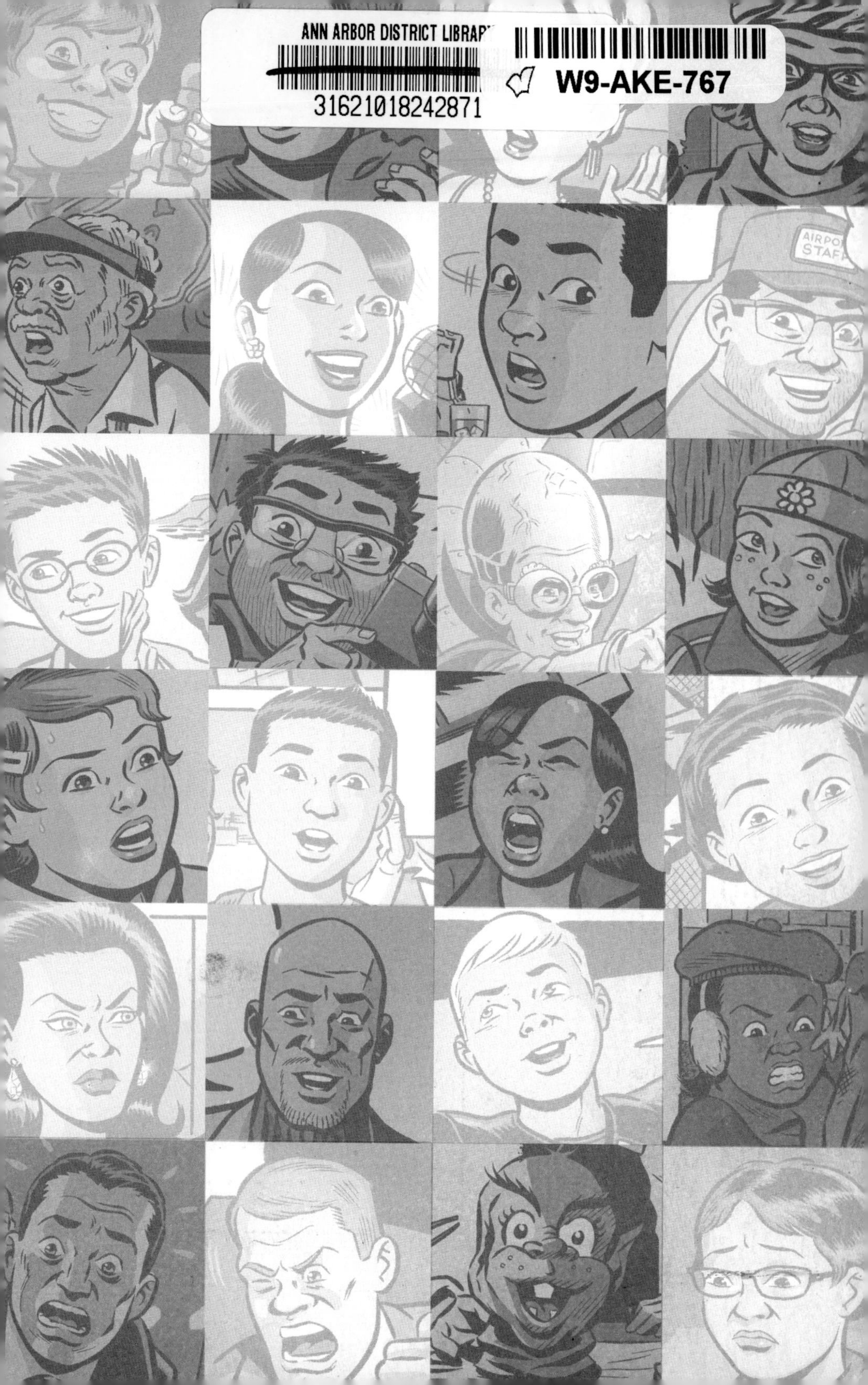

ALSO IN THE SERIES:

Max Finder Mystery Collected Casebook, Volume 1
Winner of The Association of Educational Publishers' Distinguished Achievement Award

Max Finder Mystery Collected Casebook, Volume 2

Max Finder Mystery

Collected Casebook

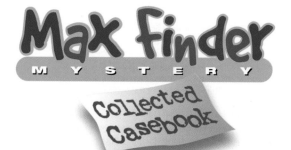

Volume 3

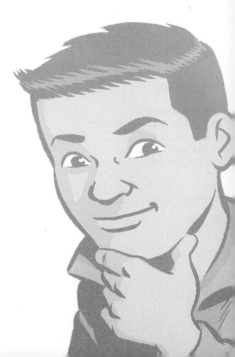

Publisher: Jennifer Canham
Editorial Director: Mary Beth Leatherdale
Editor: Katherine Dearlove
Production Editor: Larissa Byj
Production Assistant: Kathy Ko

Design: John Lightfoot/Lightfoot Art & Design Inc.

Puzzle text: Maria Birmingham
Puzzle illustrations: John Lightfoot
Comic colouring: Peter Dawes (p. 23, 29, 41, 57, 63, 69); Chris Stone (p. 11, 17, 35, 49)

Thanks to Craig Battle, David Field, Angela Keenlyside, Barb Kelly, Paul Markowski,
Susan Sinclair, Janice Weaver, Deb Yea, and Lesley Zimic.

We gratefully acknowledge the financial support of the Government of Canada through
the Book Publishing Industry Development Program (BPIDP) for our publishing activities.

Conseil des Arts   Canada Council
du Canada   for the Arts

Library and Archives Canada Cataloguing in Publication

O'Donnell, Liam, 1970-
    Max Finder mystery : collected casebook / Liam O'Donnell, Michael Cho.

ISBN 978-2-89579-116-4 (v. 1)
ISBN 978-2-89579-121-8 (v. 2)
ISBN 978-2-89579-149-2 (v. 3)

1. Detective and mystery comic books, strips, etc.--Juvenile fiction.
2. Mystery games--Juvenile fiction. 1. Bandes dessinées policières--Romans,
nouvelles, etc. pour la jeunesse. 2. Jeux de déduction--Romans, nouvelles,
etc. pour la jeunesse. I. Cho, Michael. II. Title.

PN6733.O36M38 2006   j741.5'971   C2006-903300-5
PN6733*

Printed in Canada

Owlkids Publishing
10 Lower Spadina Ave., Suite 400
Toronto, Ontario M5V 2Z2
Ph: 416-340-2700
Fax: 416-340-9769

Publisher of

chirp   chickaDEE   OWL

www.owlkids.com

Max Finder Mystery

Collected Casebook

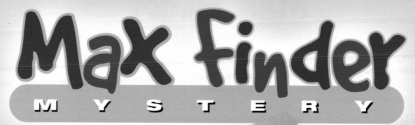

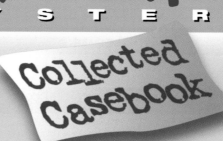

Volume 3

Liam O'Donnell

Michael Cho

Owl kids

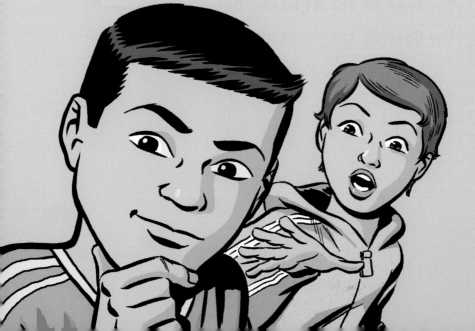

Max Finder Mystery

Collected Casebook

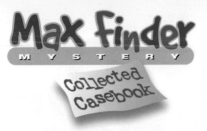

Contents

Cases

Max Finder Mystery Collected Casebook

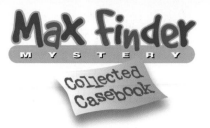

Contents

Puzzles

Extra Stuff

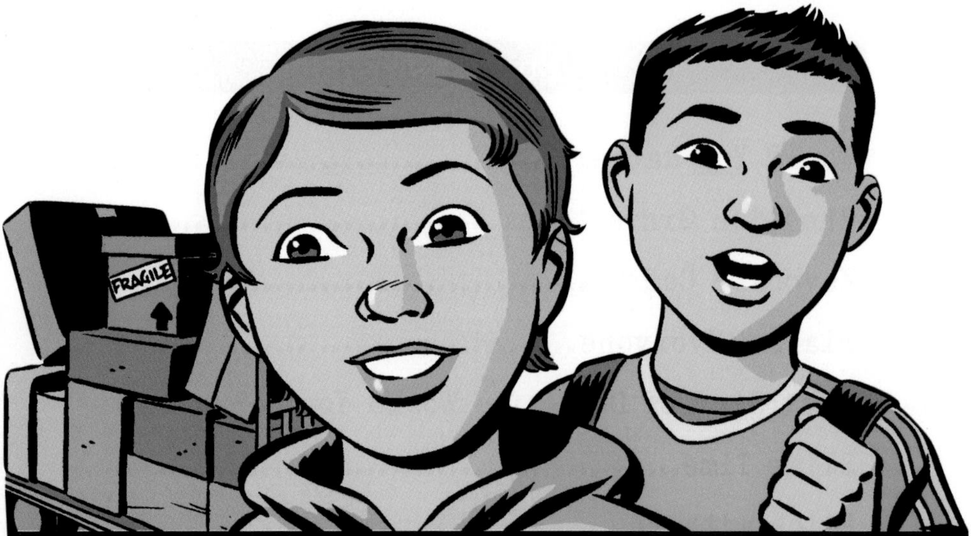
FRAGILE

Collected Casebook - Volume 3

HEY, MYSTERY FANS!

Welcome to the **Max Finder Mystery Collected Casebook, Volume 3!** Alison and I are really excited to bring you ten of the best mysteries to hit our hometown of Whispering Meadows.

From the **Back-to-School Sneak** to the **Screaming Screening**, each mysterious comic is crammed with clues, stuffed with suspects, and riddled with enough red herrings to keep you guessing until the last panel. We've done all the legwork, but solving the mystery is up to you! Read the mysteries, follow the clues, and try to crack the case. All the solutions are at the back of the book. But remember: real detectives never peek.

So, fire up your mystery radar and get solving!

Max

P.S. Check out the BONUS puzzles and the Writer's Notebook, too!

The Case of the...

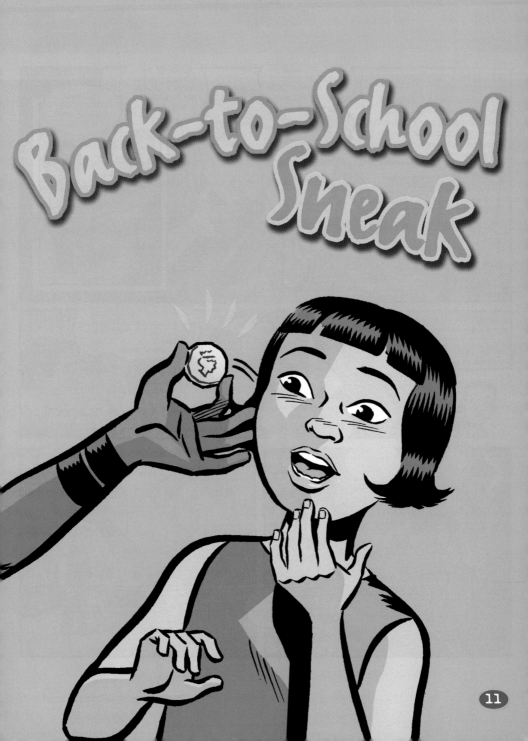

Back-to-School Sneak

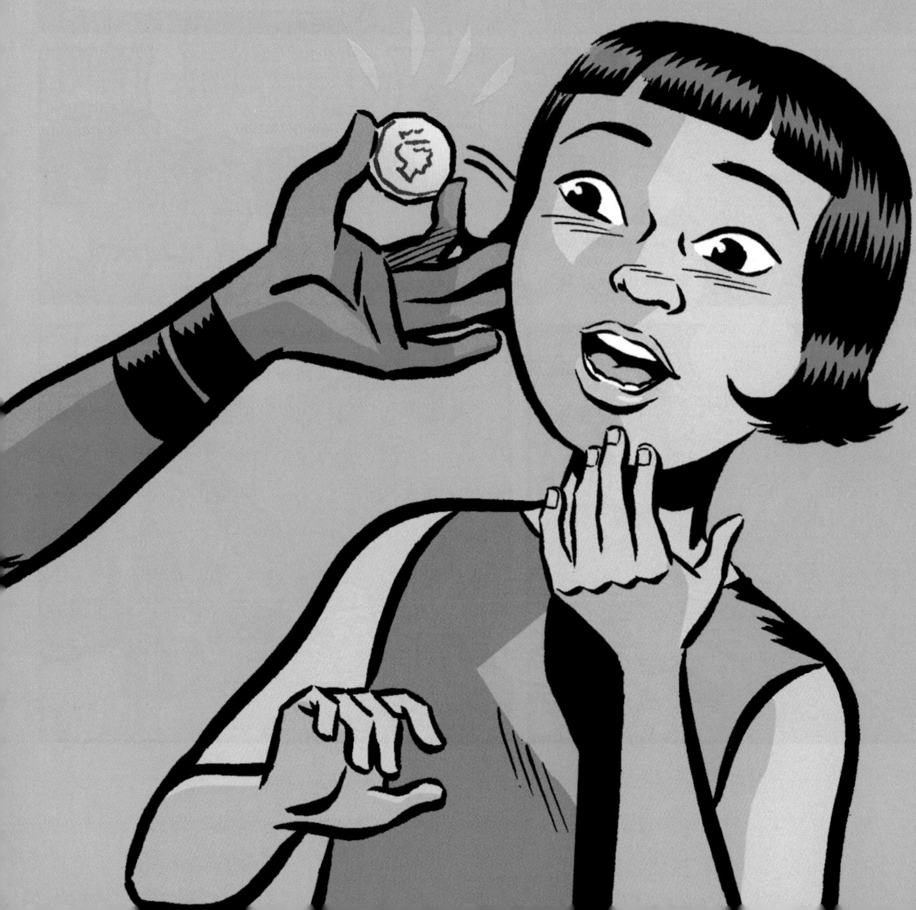

The Case of the Back-to-School Sneak

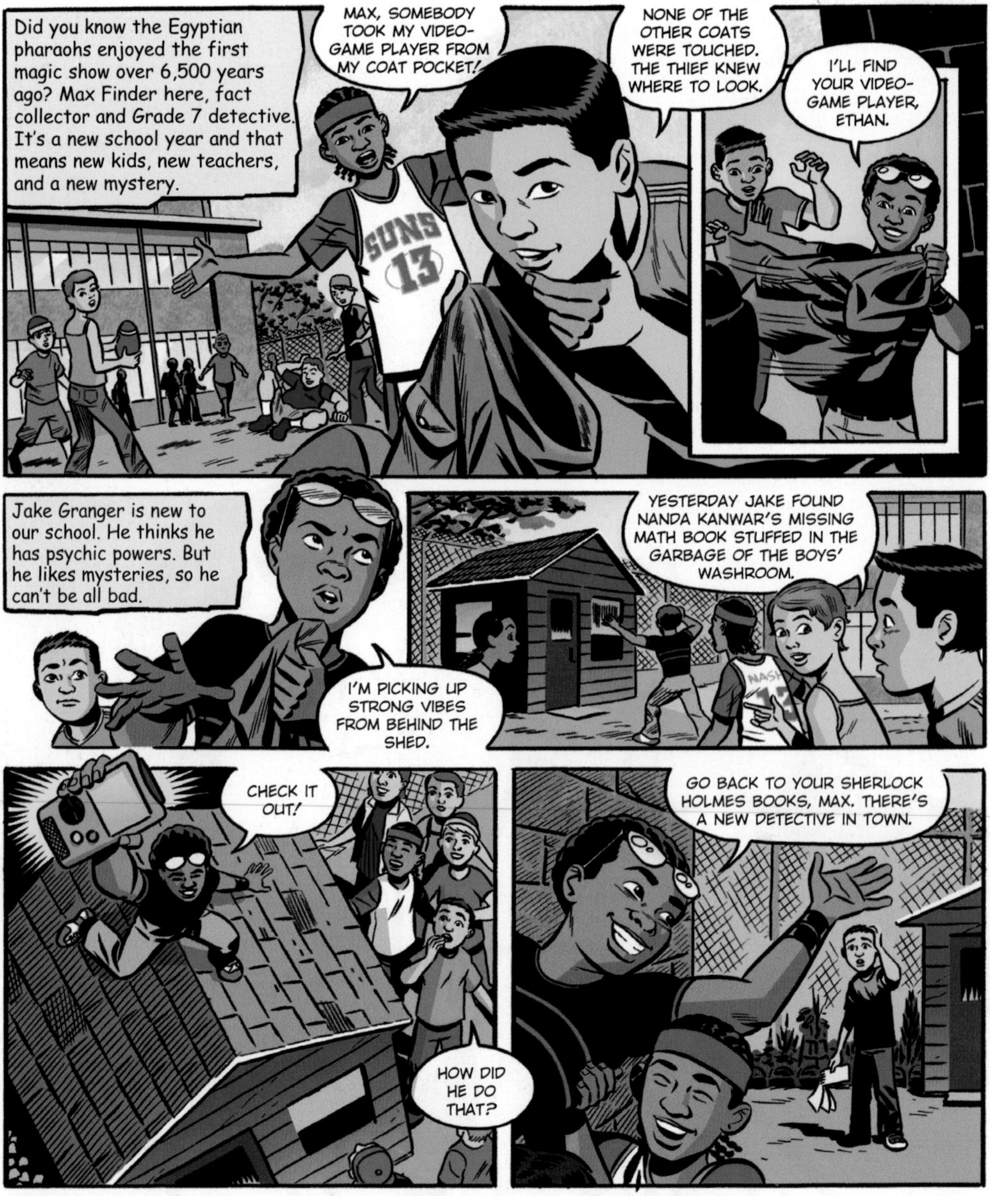

Did you know the Egyptian pharaohs enjoyed the first magic show over 6,500 years ago? Max Finder here, fact collector and Grade 7 detective. It's a new school year and that means new kids, new teachers, and a new mystery.
MAX, SOMEBODY TOOK MY VIDEO-GAME PLAYER FROM MY COAT POCKET!
NONE OF THE OTHER COATS WERE TOUCHED. THE THIEF KNEW WHERE TO LOOK.
I'LL FIND YOUR VIDEO-GAME PLAYER, ETHAN.
SUNS 13
Jake Granger is new to our school. He thinks he has psychic powers. But he likes mysteries, so he can't be all bad.
I'M PICKING UP STRONG VIBES FROM BEHIND THE SHED.
YESTERDAY JAKE FOUND NANDA KANWAR'S MISSING MATH BOOK STUFFED IN THE GARBAGE OF THE BOYS' WASHROOM.
CHECK IT OUT!
HOW DID HE DO THAT?
GO BACK TO YOUR SHERLOCK HOLMES BOOKS, MAX. THERE'S A NEW DETECTIVE IN TOWN.

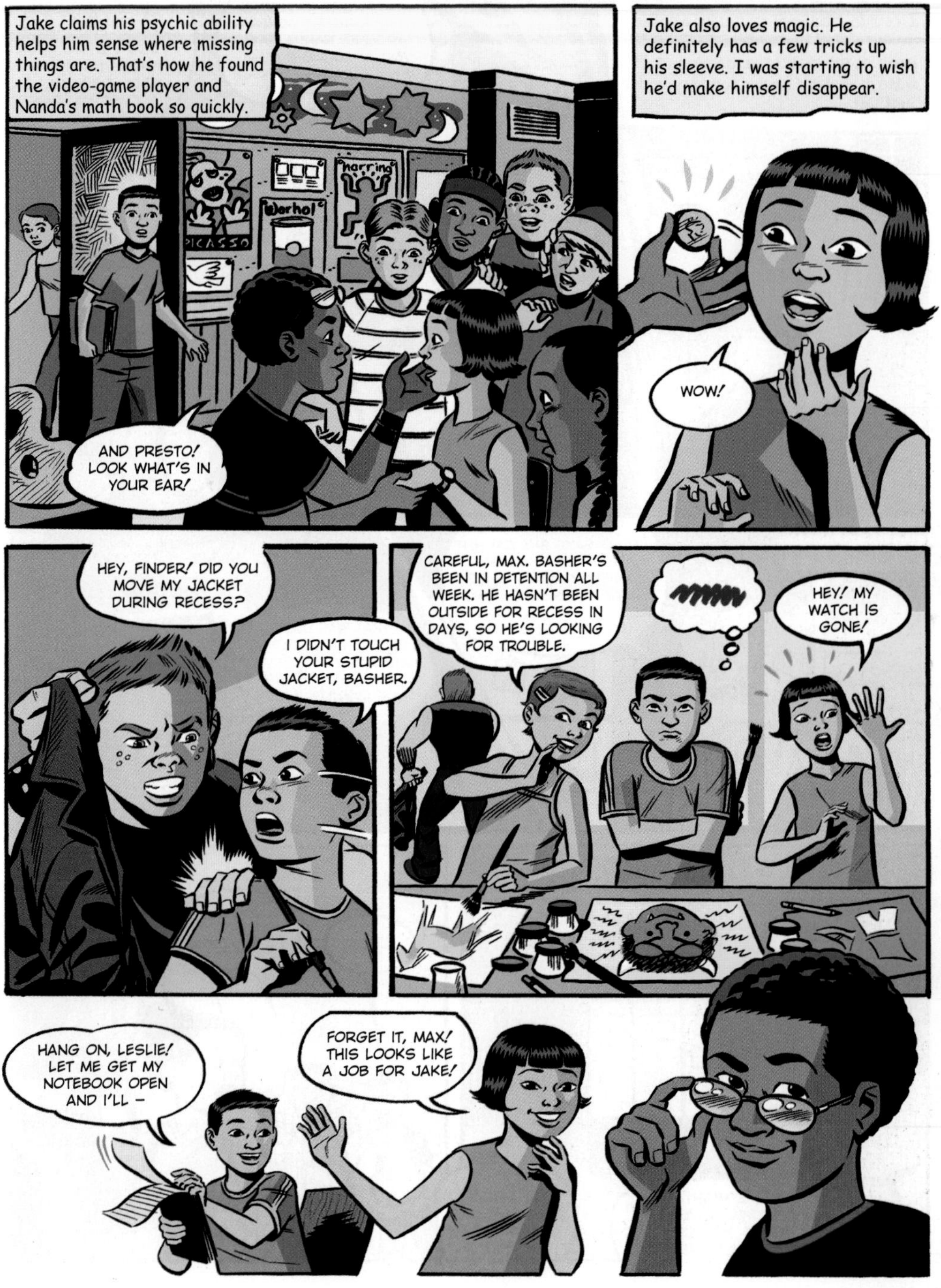
Jake claims his psychic ability helps him sense where missing things are. That's how he found the video-game player and Nanda's math book so quickly.
AND PRESTO! LOOK WHAT'S IN YOUR EAR!
Jake also loves magic. He definitely has a few tricks up his sleeve. I was starting to wish he'd make himself disappear.
WOW!
HEY, FINDER! DID YOU MOVE MY JACKET DURING RECESS?
I DIDN'T TOUCH YOUR STUPID JACKET, BASHER.
CAREFUL, MAX. BASHER'S BEEN IN DETENTION ALL WEEK. HE HASN'T BEEN OUTSIDE FOR RECESS IN DAYS, SO HE'S LOOKING FOR TROUBLE.
HEY! MY WATCH IS GONE!
HANG ON, LESLIE! LET ME GET MY NOTEBOOK OPEN AND I'LL –
FORGET IT, MAX! THIS LOOKS LIKE A JOB FOR JAKE!

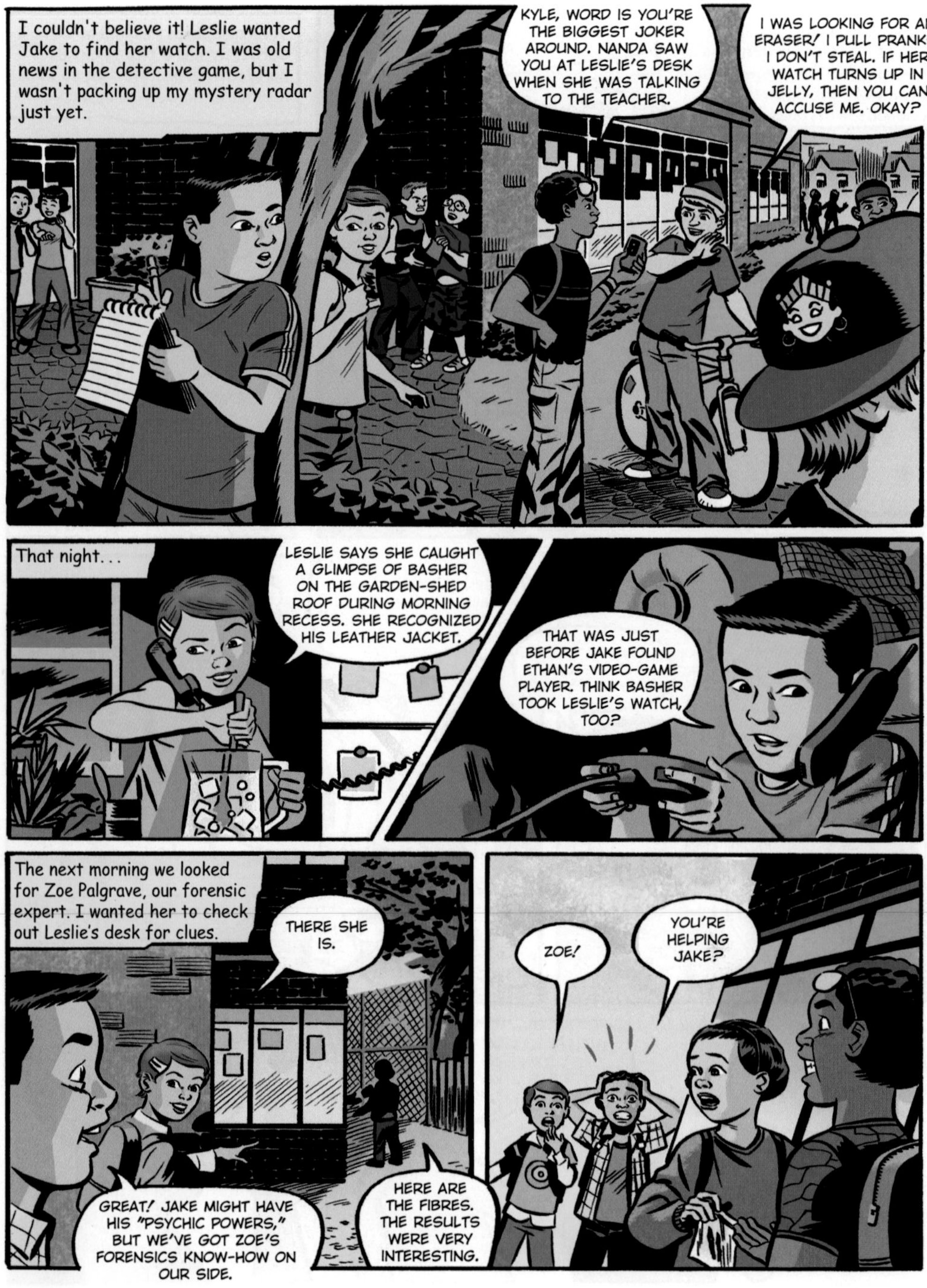

I couldn't believe it! Leslie wanted Jake to find her watch. I was old news in the detective game, but I wasn't packing up my mystery radar just yet.
KYLE, WORD IS YOU'RE THE BIGGEST JOKER AROUND. NANDA SAW YOU AT LESLIE'S DESK WHEN SHE WAS TALKING TO THE TEACHER.
I WAS LOOKING FOR AN ERASER! I PULL PRANKS, I DON'T STEAL. IF HER WATCH TURNS UP IN JELLY, THEN YOU CAN ACCUSE ME. OKAY?
That night...
LESLIE SAYS SHE CAUGHT A GLIMPSE OF BASHER ON THE GARDEN-SHED ROOF DURING MORNING RECESS. SHE RECOGNIZED HIS LEATHER JACKET.
THAT WAS JUST BEFORE JAKE FOUND ETHAN'S VIDEO-GAME PLAYER. THINK BASHER TOOK LESLIE'S WATCH, TOO?
The next morning we looked for Zoe Palgrave, our forensic expert. I wanted her to check out Leslie's desk for clues.
THERE SHE IS.
GREAT! JAKE MIGHT HAVE HIS "PSYCHIC POWERS," BUT WE'VE GOT ZOE'S FORENSICS KNOW-HOW ON OUR SIDE.
HERE ARE THE FIBRES. THE RESULTS WERE VERY INTERESTING.
ZOE!
YOU'RE HELPING JAKE?

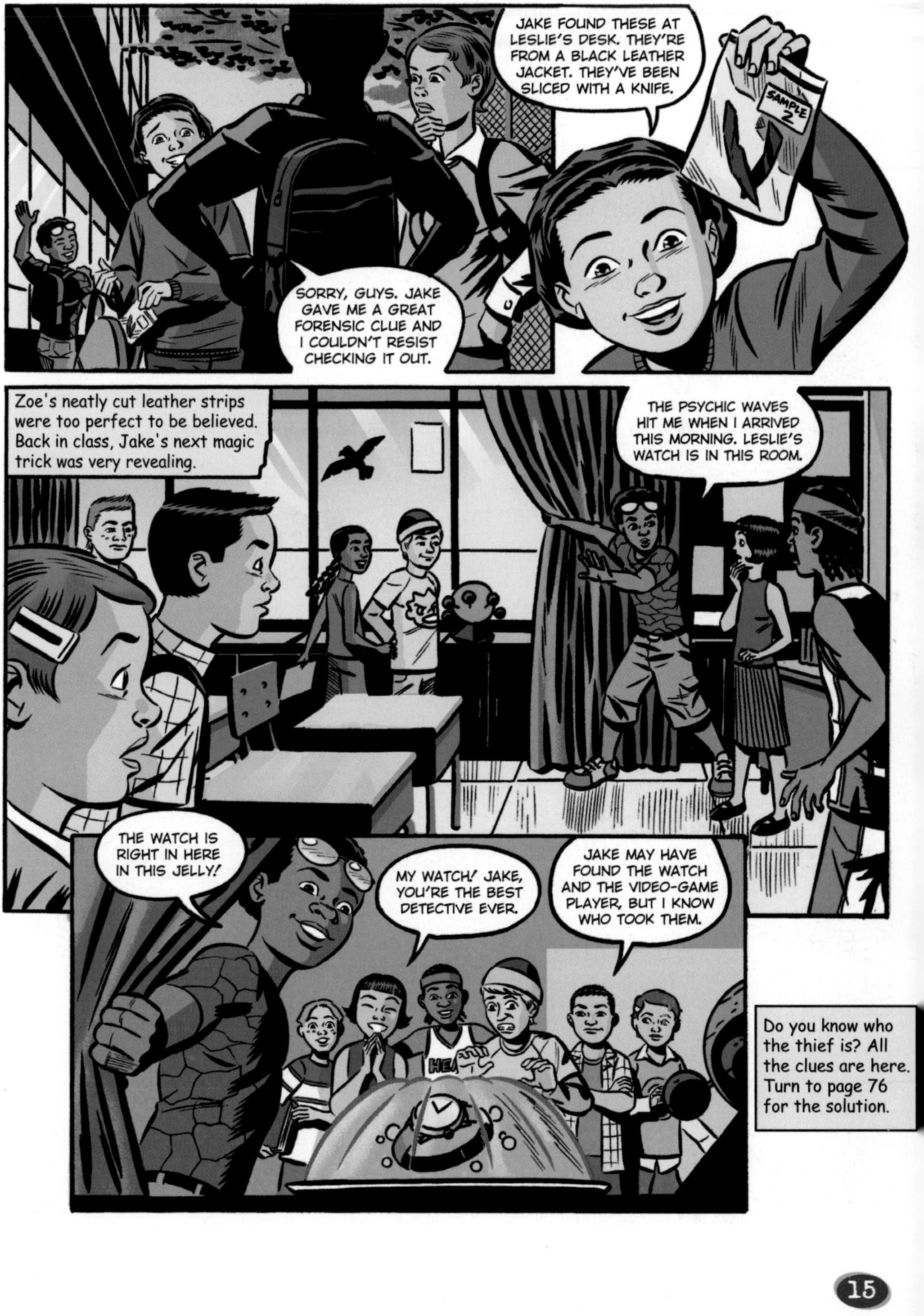
JAKE FOUND THESE AT LESLIE'S DESK. THEY'RE FROM A BLACK LEATHER JACKET. THEY'VE BEEN SLICED WITH A KNIFE.
SAMPLE 2
SORRY, GUYS. JAKE GAVE ME A GREAT FORENSIC CLUE AND I COULDN'T RESIST CHECKING IT OUT.
Zoe's neatly cut leather strips were too perfect to be believed. Back in class, Jake's next magic trick was very revealing.
THE PSYCHIC WAVES HIT ME WHEN I ARRIVED THIS MORNING. LESLIE'S WATCH IS IN THIS ROOM.
THE WATCH IS RIGHT IN HERE IN THIS JELLY!
MY WATCH! JAKE, YOU'RE THE BEST DETECTIVE EVER.
JAKE MAY HAVE FOUND THE WATCH AND THE VIDEO-GAME PLAYER, BUT I KNOW WHO TOOK THEM.

Do you know who the thief is? All the clues are here. Turn to page 76 for the solution.

Would You Rather?

Back-to-School Edition

Answer the mind-bending questions below.
Quiz your friends and family, too!

▸ Would you rather be the teacher's pet or the class clown?

▸ Would you rather fly to school with your own jetpack or travel through secret underground tunnels?

▸ Would you rather have straight A's or score the winning goal at the city-wide soccer tournament?

▸ Would you rather take a class trip to the top of Mount Everest or to a deserted island in the South Pacific?

▸ Would you rather be the school band's star tuba player or the spelling bee champ?

▸ Would you rather be able to pass invisible notes in class or finish your homework in three minutes every day?

▸ Would you rather be in the same class as your best friend or your fave teacher?

▸ Would you rather ace tests with your photographic memory or win track meets with your Olympic speed?

▸ Would you rather have something new to wear every day or something new to eat for lunch every day?

▸ Would you rather spin the tunes at the school dance or star in the school play?

Haunted Haunted House

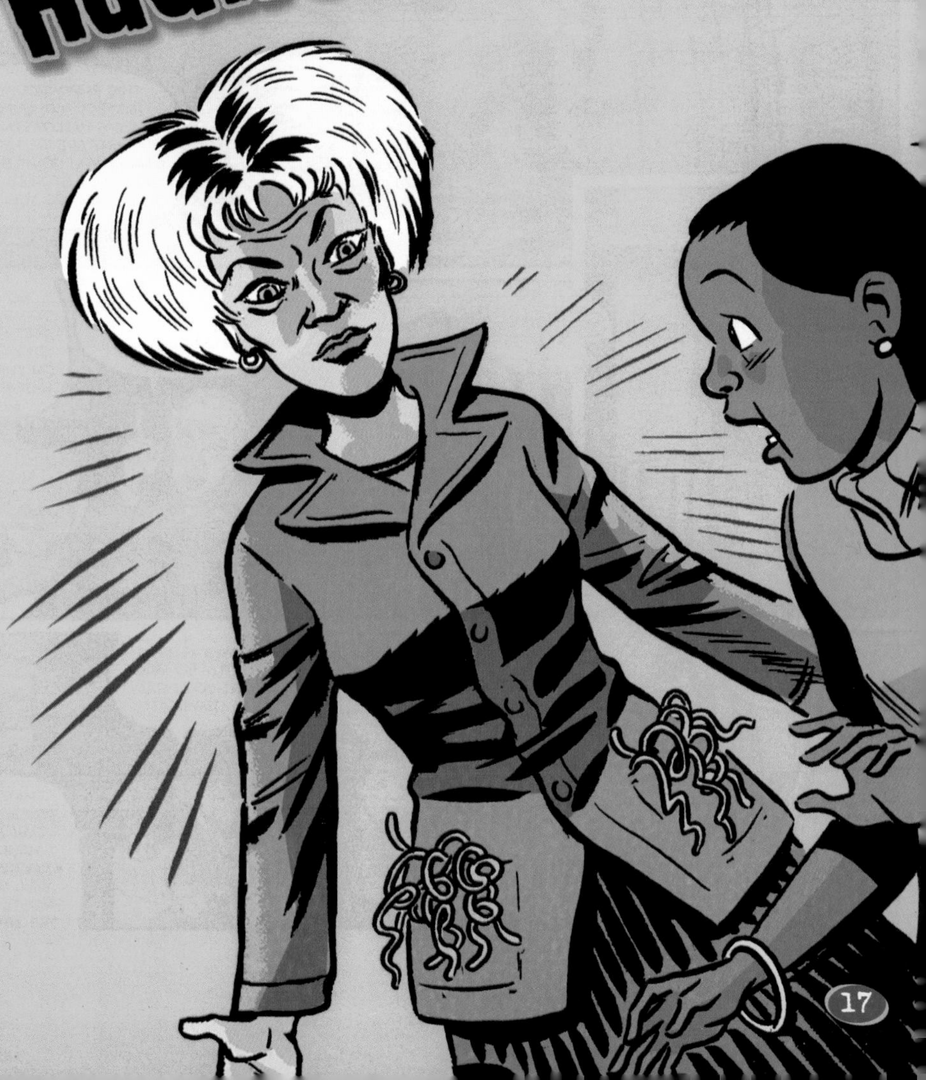

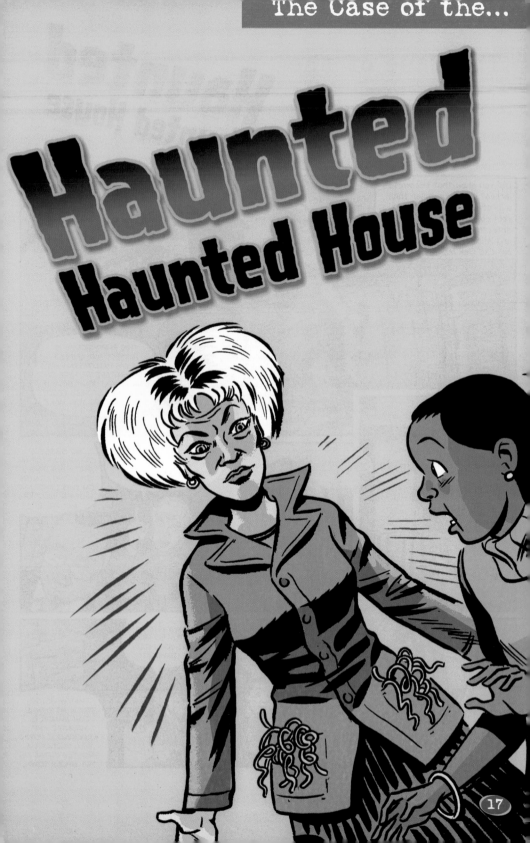

The Case of the Haunted Haunted House

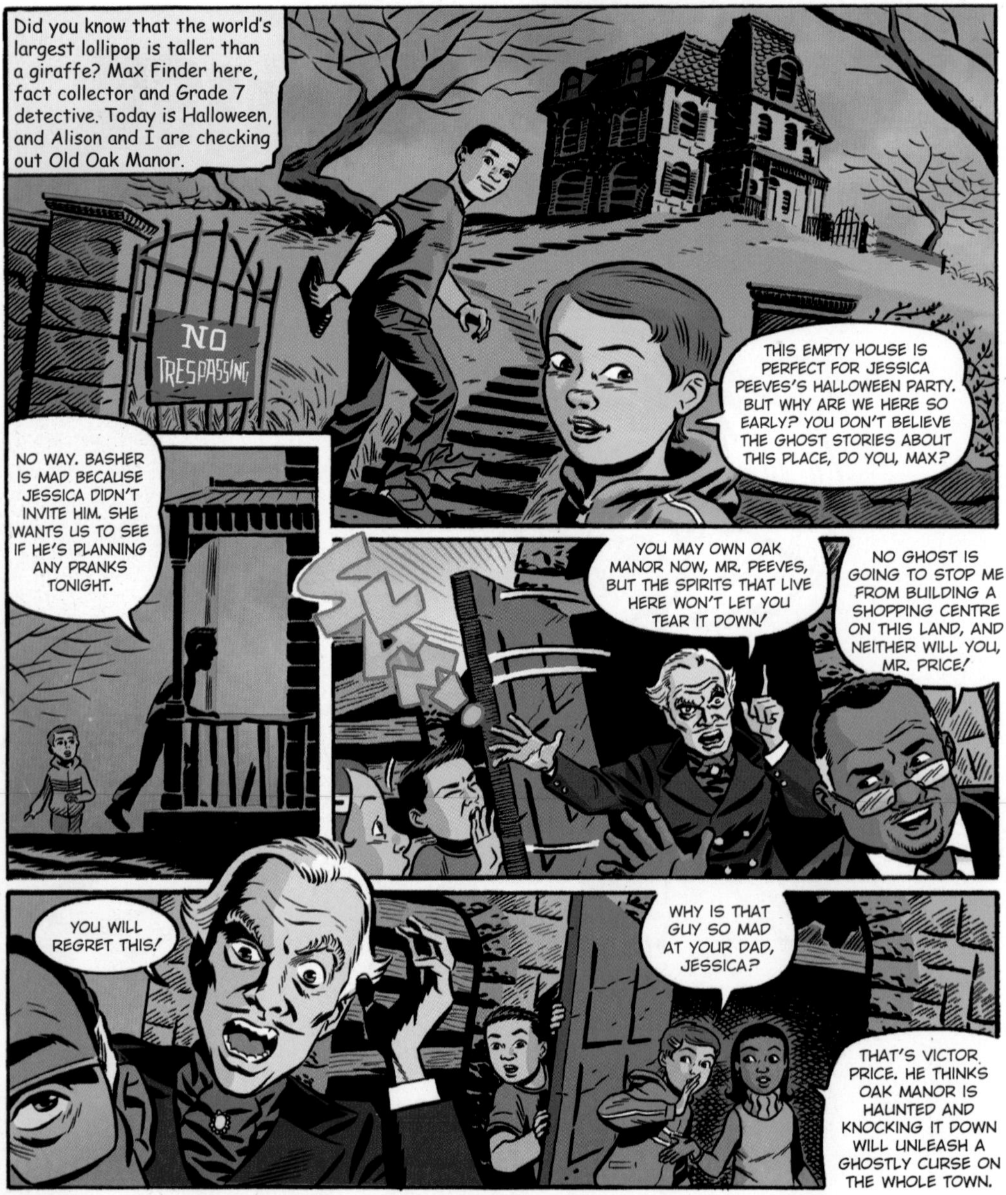

Did you know that the world's largest lollipop is taller than a giraffe? Max Finder here, fact collector and Grade 7 detective. Today is Halloween, and Alison and I are checking out Old Oak Manor.
NO TRESPASSING
THIS EMPTY HOUSE IS PERFECT FOR JESSICA PEEVES'S HALLOWEEN PARTY. BUT WHY ARE WE HERE SO EARLY? YOU DON'T BELIEVE THE GHOST STORIES ABOUT THIS PLACE, DO YOU, MAX?
NO WAY. BASHER IS MAD BECAUSE JESSICA DIDN'T INVITE HIM. SHE WANTS US TO SEE IF HE'S PLANNING ANY PRANKS TONIGHT.
YOU MAY OWN OAK MANOR NOW, MR. PEEVES, BUT THE SPIRITS THAT LIVE HERE WON'T LET YOU TEAR IT DOWN!
NO GHOST IS GOING TO STOP ME FROM BUILDING A SHOPPING CENTRE ON THIS LAND, AND NEITHER WILL YOU, MR. PRICE!
YOU WILL REGRET THIS!
WHY IS THAT GUY SO MAD AT YOUR DAD, JESSICA?
THAT'S VICTOR PRICE. HE THINKS OAK MANOR IS HAUNTED AND KNOCKING IT DOWN WILL UNLEASH A GHOSTLY CURSE ON THE WHOLE TOWN.

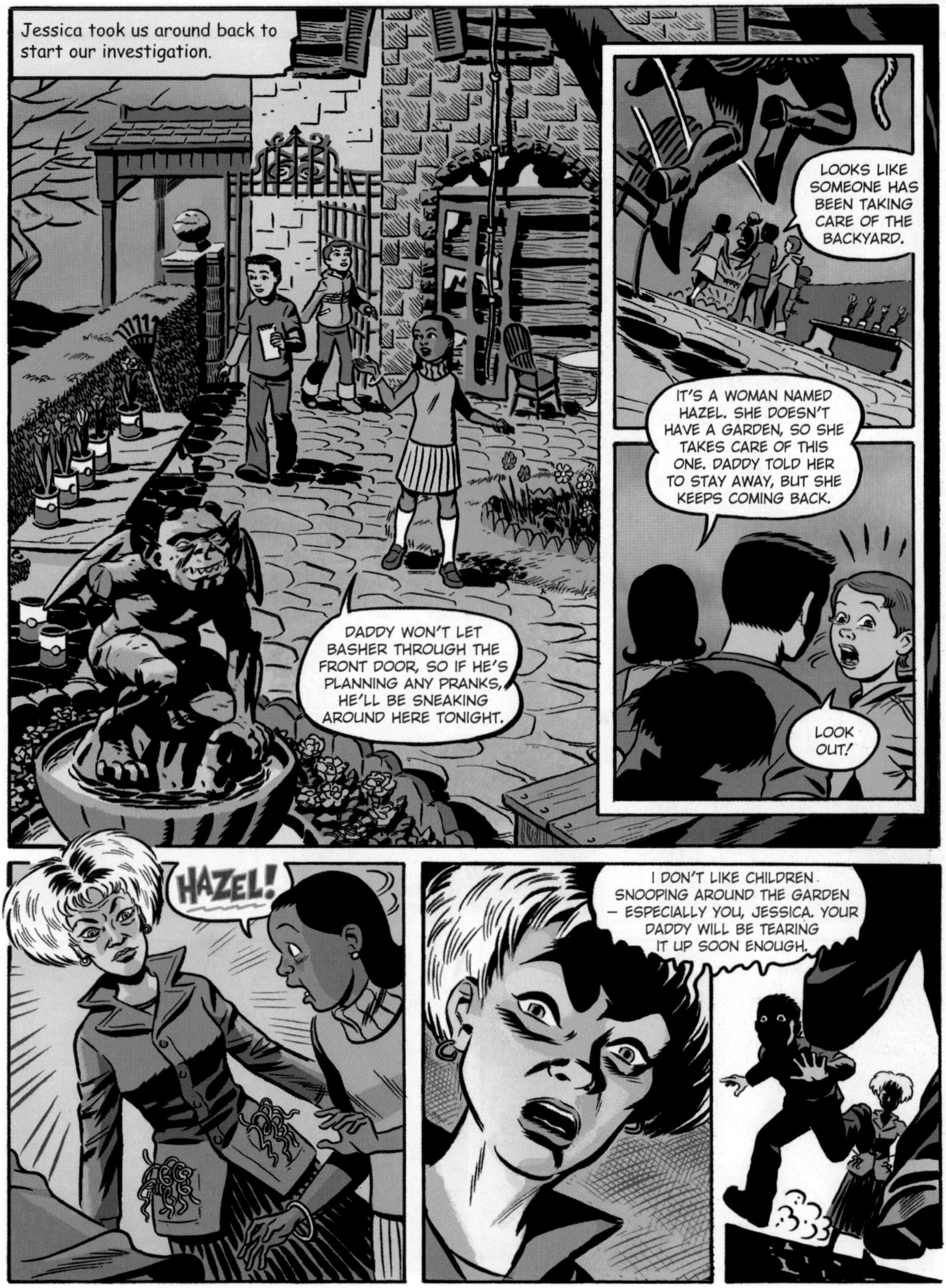
Jessica took us around back to start our investigation.
DADDY WON'T LET BASHER THROUGH THE FRONT DOOR, SO IF HE'S PLANNING ANY PRANKS, HE'LL BE SNEAKING AROUND HERE TONIGHT.
LOOKS LIKE SOMEONE HAS BEEN TAKING CARE OF THE BACKYARD.
IT'S A WOMAN NAMED HAZEL. SHE DOESN'T HAVE A GARDEN, SO SHE TAKES CARE OF THIS ONE. DADDY TOLD HER TO STAY AWAY, BUT SHE KEEPS COMING BACK.
LOOK OUT!
HAZEL!
I DON'T LIKE CHILDREN SNOOPING AROUND THE GARDEN – ESPECIALLY YOU, JESSICA. YOUR DADDY WILL BE TEARING IT UP SOON ENOUGH.

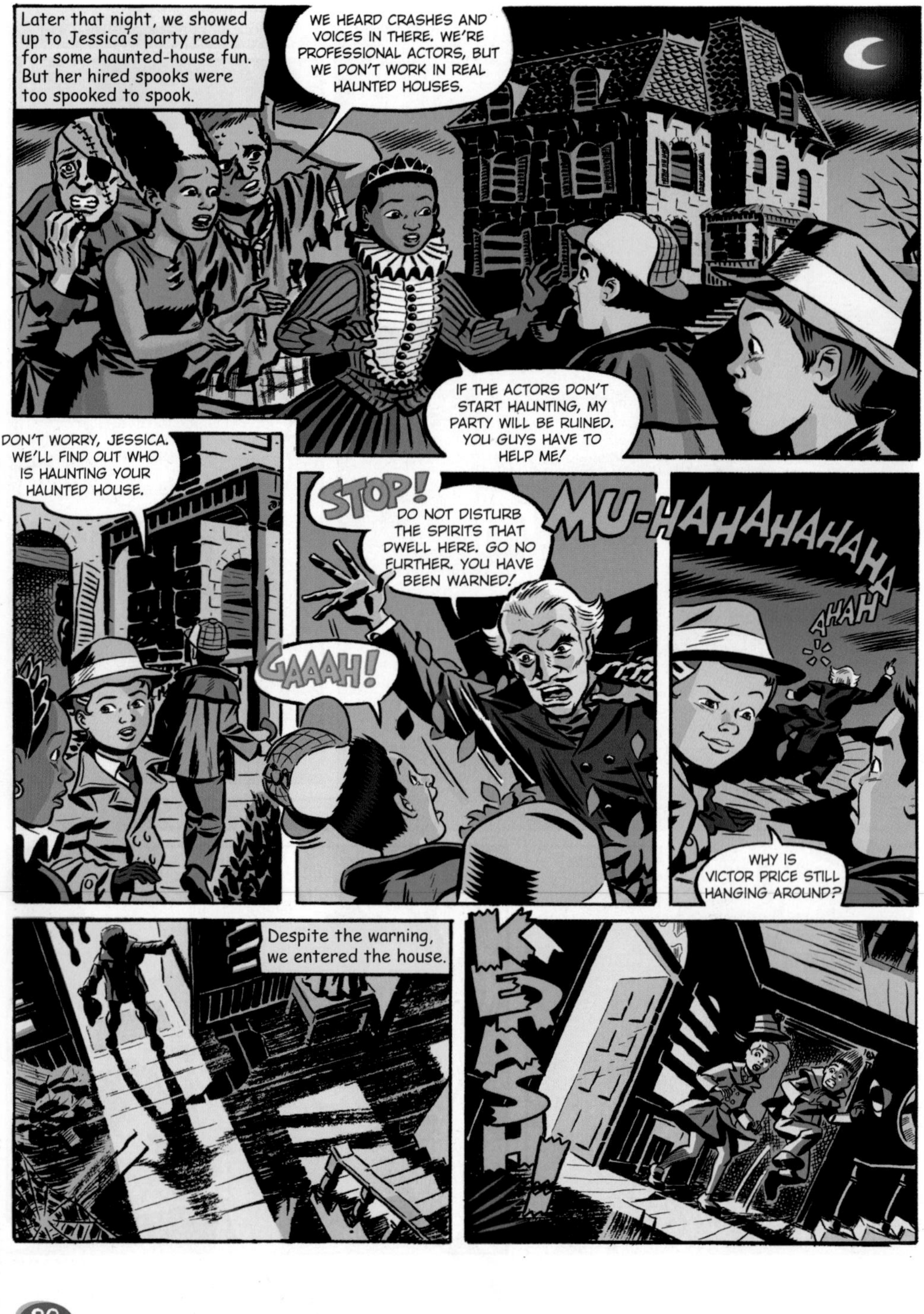
Later that night, we showed up to Jessica's party ready for some haunted-house fun. But her hired spooks were too spooked to spook.
WE HEARD CRASHES AND VOICES IN THERE. WE'RE PROFESSIONAL ACTORS, BUT WE DON'T WORK IN REAL HAUNTED HOUSES.
IF THE ACTORS DON'T START HAUNTING, MY PARTY WILL BE RUINED. YOU GUYS HAVE TO HELP ME!
DON'T WORRY, JESSICA. WE'LL FIND OUT WHO IS HAUNTING YOUR HAUNTED HOUSE.
STOP!
DO NOT DISTURB THE SPIRITS THAT DWELL HERE. GO NO FURTHER. YOU HAVE BEEN WARNED!
GAAAH!
MU-HAHAHAHAHAHAHAHAH
WHY IS VICTOR PRICE STILL HANGING AROUND?
Despite the warning, we entered the house.
KERASH!

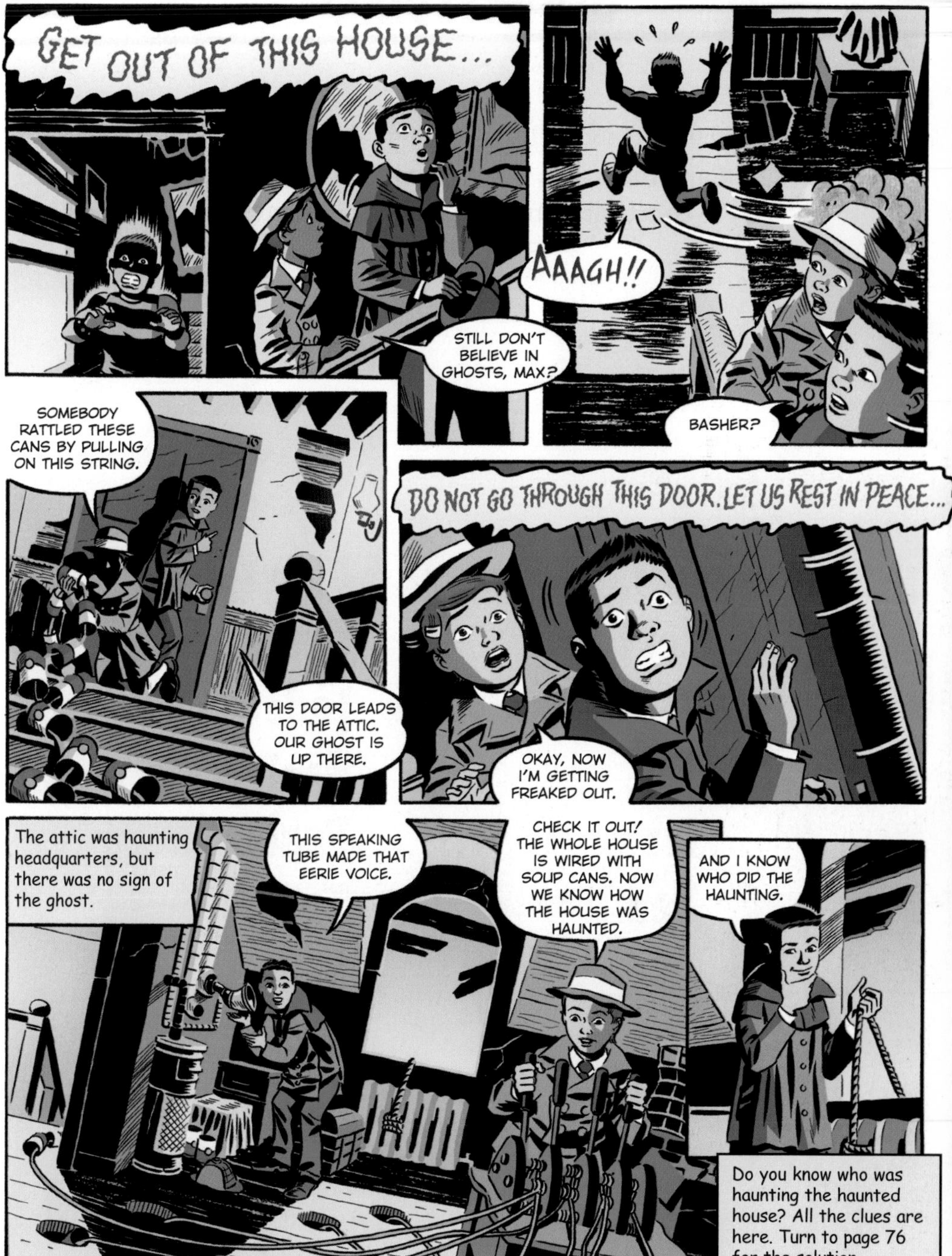
GET OUT OF THIS HOUSE...
STILL DON'T BELIEVE IN GHOSTS, MAX?
AAAGH!!
BASHER?
SOMEBODY RATTLED THESE CANS BY PULLING ON THIS STRING.
THIS DOOR LEADS TO THE ATTIC. OUR GHOST IS UP THERE.
DO NOT GO THROUGH THIS DOOR. LET US REST IN PEACE...
OKAY, NOW I'M GETTING FREAKED OUT.
The attic was haunting headquarters, but there was no sign of the ghost.
THIS SPEAKING TUBE MADE THAT EERIE VOICE.
CHECK IT OUT! THE WHOLE HOUSE IS WIRED WITH SOUP CANS. NOW WE KNOW HOW THE HOUSE WAS HAUNTED.
AND I KNOW WHO DID THE HAUNTING.
Do you know who was haunting the haunted house? All the clues are here. Turn to page 76 for the solution.

Ghoulish
Gravestones

Jessica's dad set up funny gravestones at the Halloween party.

**Can you match the first and last names to
come up with the phony full names?**

M.T.	Ghost
Left B.	Dead
Ricky D.	Lader
R.U.	Parted
Izzy	Peace
Dee	Toomb
C.U.	Bones
Ima	Hynde
Rustin	Next

ANSWERS PAGE 84

Mars Malfunction

The Case of the Mars Malfunction

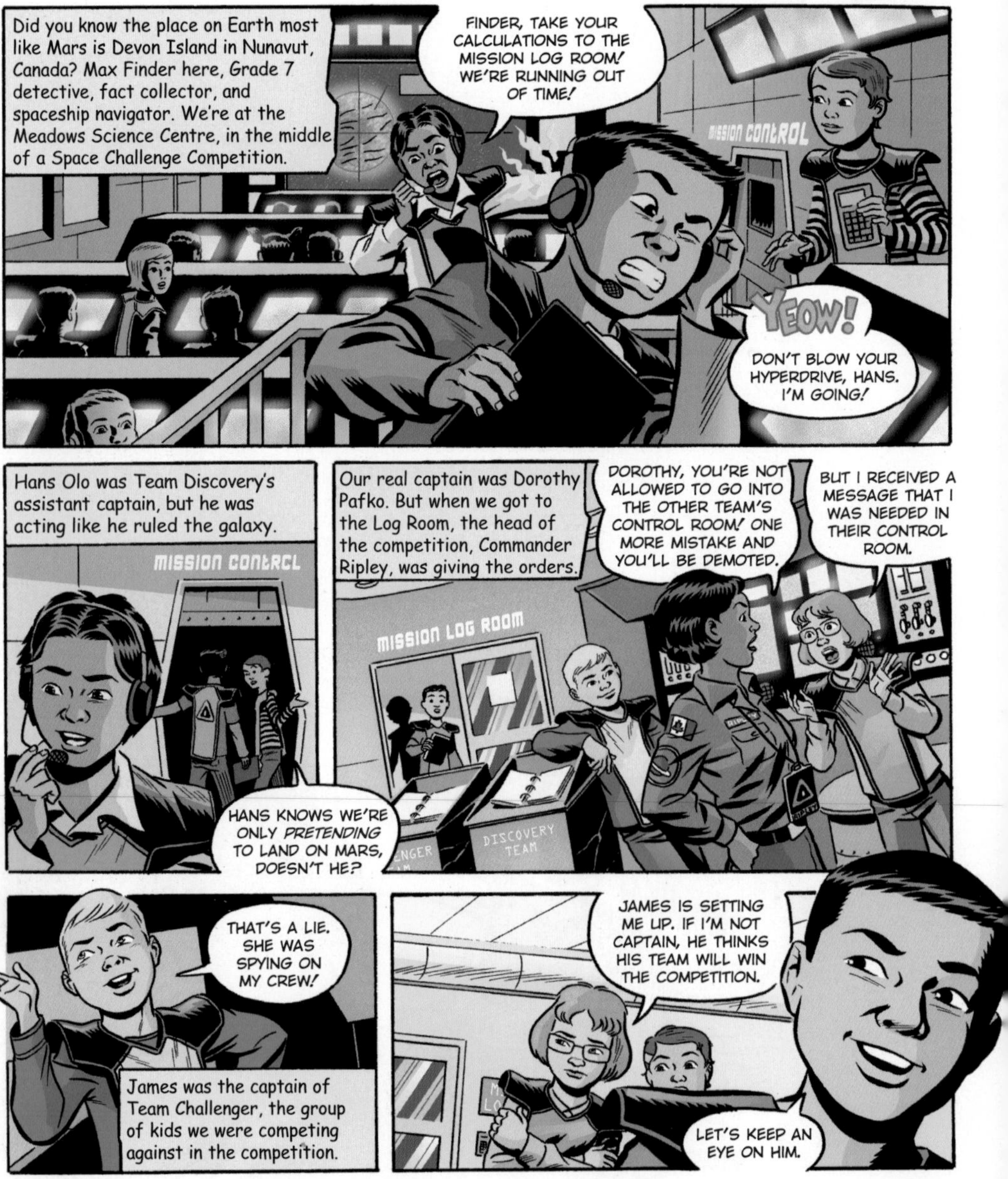

Did you know the place on Earth most like Mars is Devon Island in Nunavut, Canada? Max Finder here, Grade 7 detective, fact collector, and spaceship navigator. We're at the Meadows Science Centre, in the middle of a Space Challenge Competition.
FINDER, TAKE YOUR CALCULATIONS TO THE MISSION LOG ROOM! WE'RE RUNNING OUT OF TIME!
MISSION CONTROL
YEOW!
DON'T BLOW YOUR HYPERDRIVE, HANS. I'M GOING!
Hans Olo was Team Discovery's assistant captain, but he was acting like he ruled the galaxy.
MISSION CONTROL
HANS KNOWS WE'RE ONLY *PRETENDING* TO LAND ON MARS, DOESN'T HE?
Our real captain was Dorothy Pafko. But when we got to the Log Room, the head of the competition, Commander Ripley, was giving the orders.
MISSION LOG ROOM
DOROTHY, YOU'RE NOT ALLOWED TO GO INTO THE OTHER TEAM'S CONTROL ROOM! ONE MORE MISTAKE AND YOU'LL BE DEMOTED.
BUT I RECEIVED A MESSAGE THAT I WAS NEEDED IN THEIR CONTROL ROOM.
DISCOVERY TEAM
THAT'S A LIE. SHE WAS SPYING ON MY CREW!
James was the captain of Team Challenger, the group of kids we were competing against in the competition.
JAMES IS SETTING ME UP. IF I'M NOT CAPTAIN, HE THINKS HIS TEAM WILL WIN THE COMPETITION.
LET'S KEEP AN EYE ON HIM.

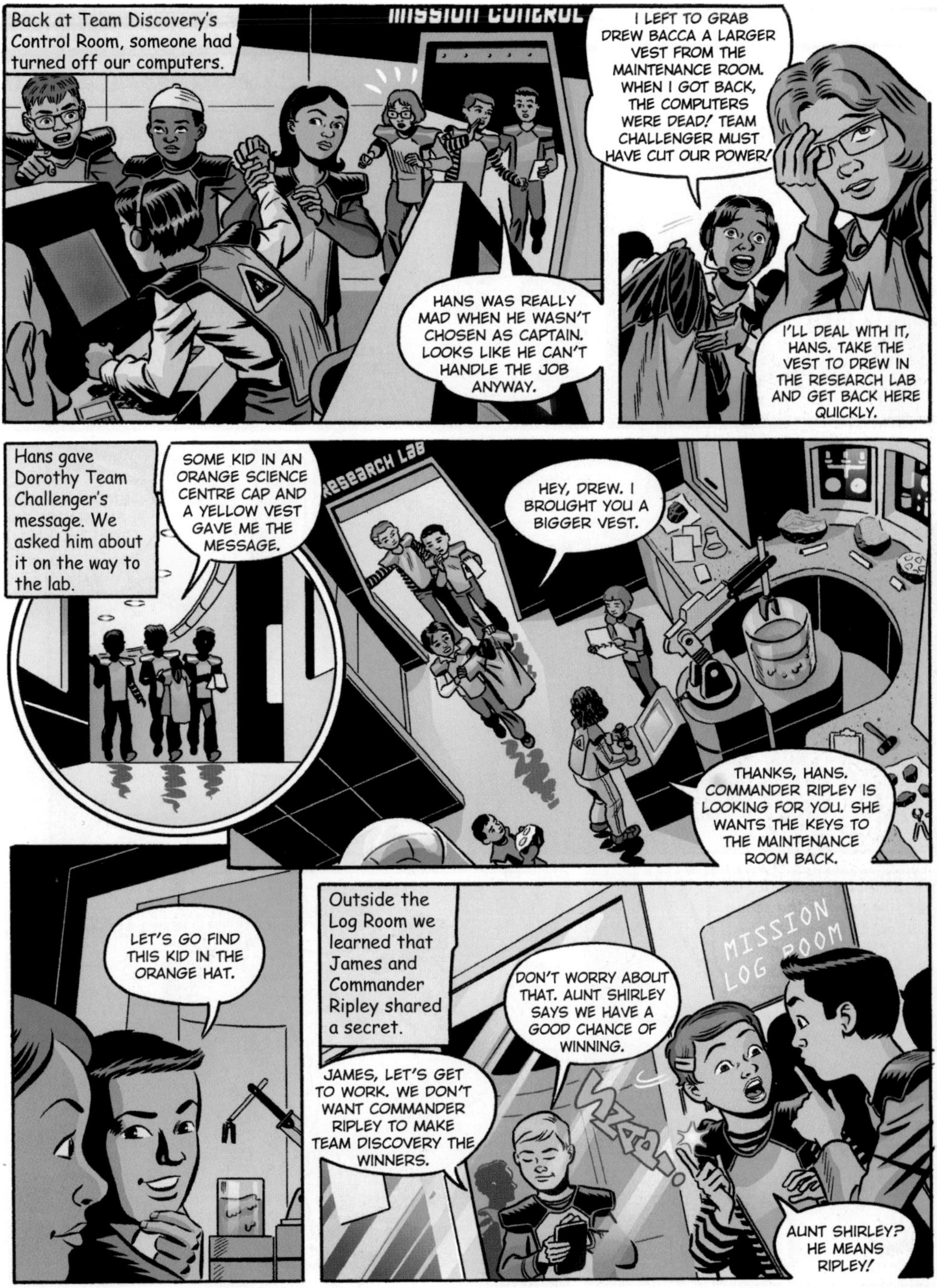
Back at Team Discovery's Control Room, someone had turned off our computers.
MISSION CONTROL
HANS WAS REALLY MAD WHEN HE WASN'T CHOSEN AS CAPTAIN. LOOKS LIKE HE CAN'T HANDLE THE JOB ANYWAY.
I LEFT TO GRAB DREW BACCA A LARGER VEST FROM THE MAINTENANCE ROOM. WHEN I GOT BACK, THE COMPUTERS WERE DEAD! TEAM CHALLENGER MUST HAVE CUT OUR POWER!
I'LL DEAL WITH IT, HANS. TAKE THE VEST TO DREW IN THE RESEARCH LAB AND GET BACK HERE QUICKLY.
Hans gave Dorothy Team Challenger's message. We asked him about it on the way to the lab.
SOME KID IN AN ORANGE SCIENCE CENTRE CAP AND A YELLOW VEST GAVE ME THE MESSAGE.
RESEARCH LAB
HEY, DREW. I BROUGHT YOU A BIGGER VEST.
THANKS, HANS. COMMANDER RIPLEY IS LOOKING FOR YOU. SHE WANTS THE KEYS TO THE MAINTENANCE ROOM BACK.
LET'S GO FIND THIS KID IN THE ORANGE HAT.
Outside the Log Room we learned that James and Commander Ripley shared a secret.
MISSION LOG ROOM
JAMES, LET'S GET TO WORK. WE DON'T WANT COMMANDER RIPLEY TO MAKE TEAM DISCOVERY THE WINNERS.
DON'T WORRY ABOUT THAT. AUNT SHIRLEY SAYS WE HAVE A GOOD CHANCE OF WINNING.
AUNT SHIRLEY? HE MEANS RIPLEY!

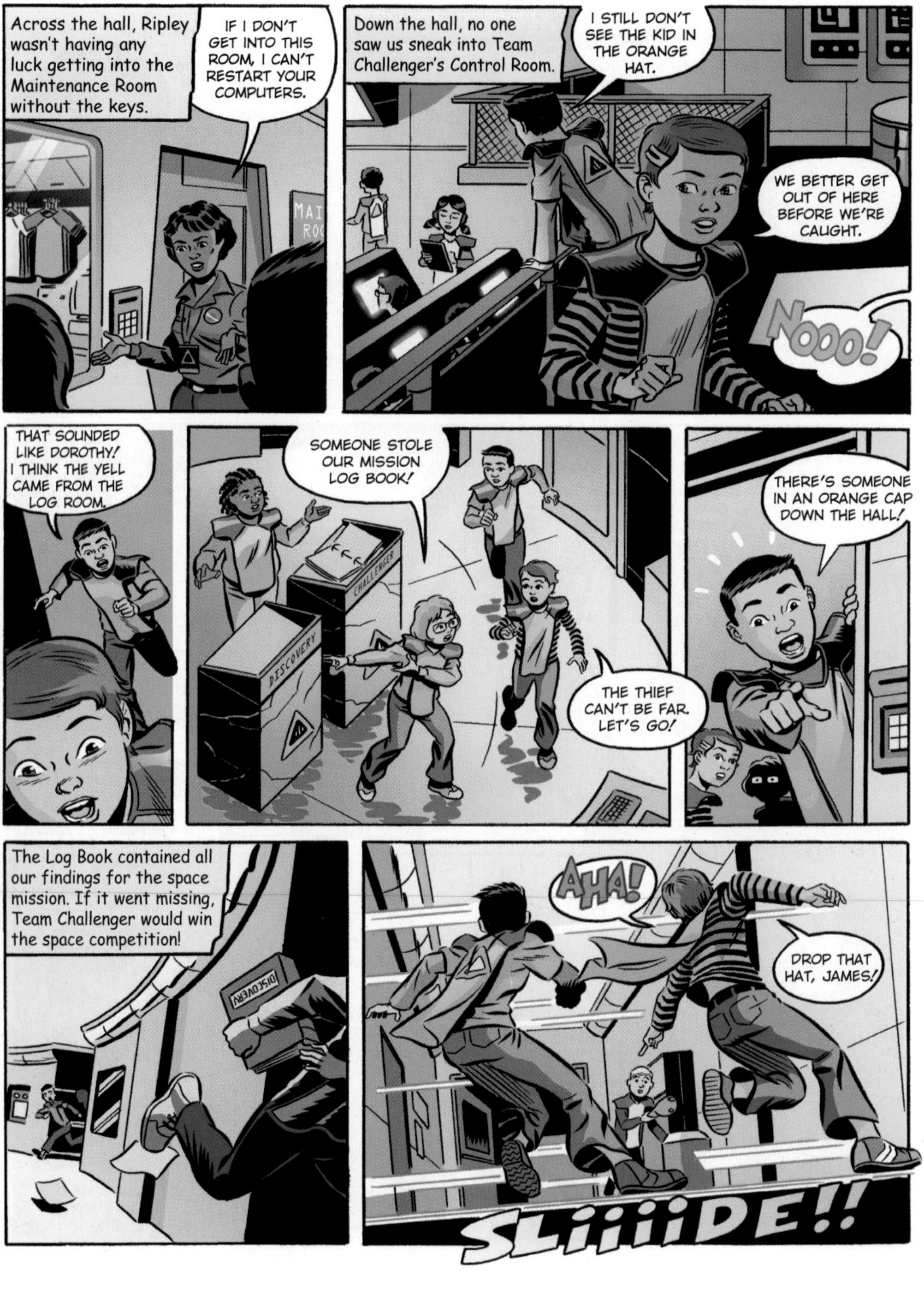
Across the hall, Ripley wasn't having any luck getting into the Maintenance Room without the keys.
IF I DON'T GET INTO THIS ROOM, I CAN'T RESTART YOUR COMPUTERS.
Down the hall, no one saw us sneak into Team Challenger's Control Room.
I STILL DON'T SEE THE KID IN THE ORANGE HAT.
WE BETTER GET OUT OF HERE BEFORE WE'RE CAUGHT.
NOOO!
THAT SOUNDED LIKE DOROTHY! I THINK THE YELL CAME FROM THE LOG ROOM.
SOMEONE STOLE OUR MISSION LOG BOOK!
CHALLENGER
DISCOVERY
THE THIEF CAN'T BE FAR. LET'S GO!
THERE'S SOMEONE IN AN ORANGE CAP DOWN THE HALL!
The Log Book contained all our findings for the space mission. If it went missing, Team Challenger would win the space competition!
DISCOVERY
AHA!
DROP THAT HAT, JAMES!
SLIiiiDE!!

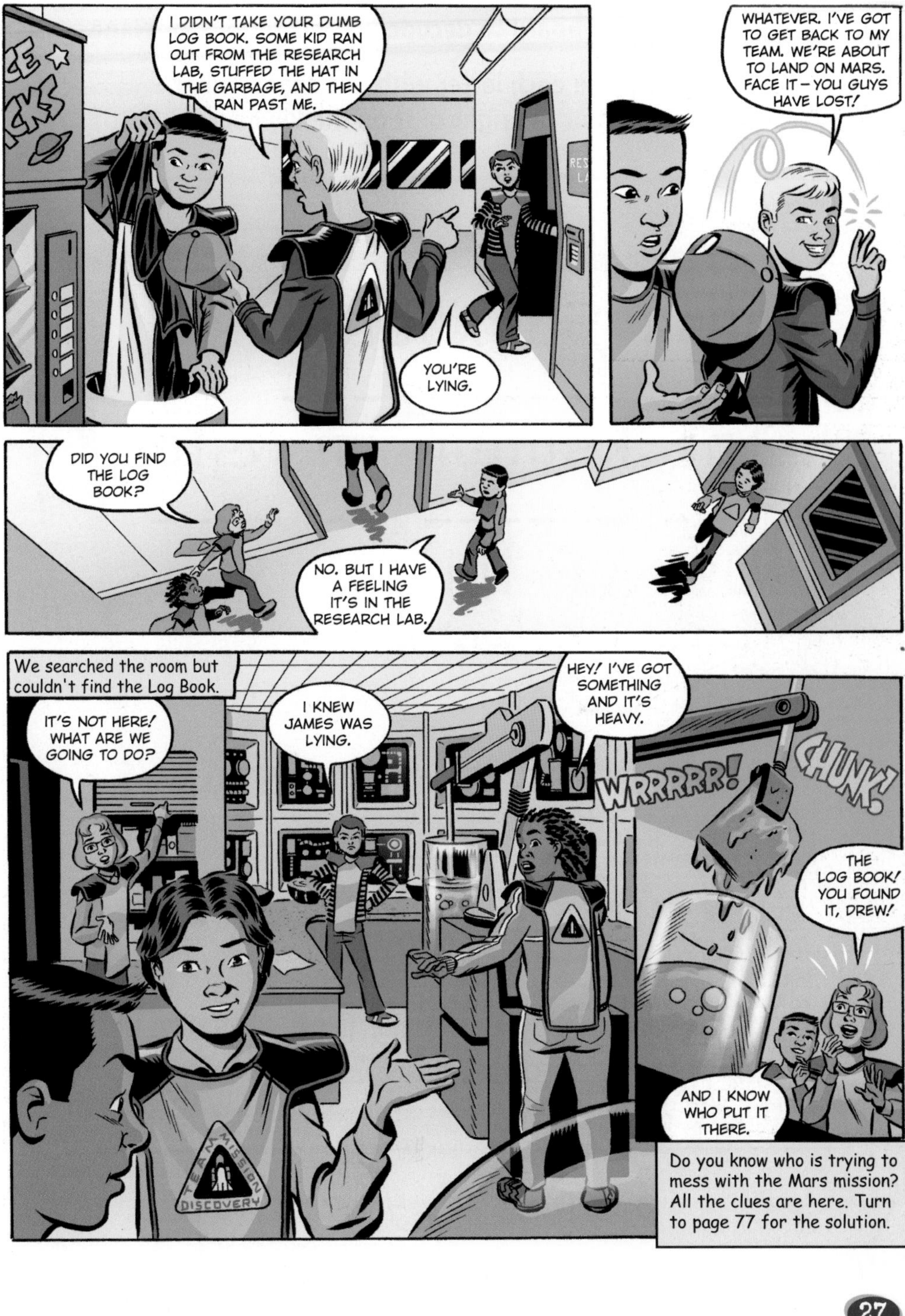
I DIDN'T TAKE YOUR DUMB LOG BOOK. SOME KID RAN OUT FROM THE RESEARCH LAB, STUFFED THE HAT IN THE GARBAGE, AND THEN RAN PAST ME.
YOU'RE LYING.
WHATEVER. I'VE GOT TO GET BACK TO MY TEAM. WE'RE ABOUT TO LAND ON MARS. FACE IT – YOU GUYS HAVE LOST!
DID YOU FIND THE LOG BOOK?
NO. BUT I HAVE A FEELING IT'S IN THE RESEARCH LAB.
We searched the room but couldn't find the Log Book.
IT'S NOT HERE! WHAT ARE WE GOING TO DO?
I KNEW JAMES WAS LYING.
HEY! I'VE GOT SOMETHING AND IT'S HEAVY.
WRRRRR!
CHUNK!
THE LOG BOOK! YOU FOUND IT, DREW!
AND I KNOW WHO PUT IT THERE.
Do you know who is trying to mess with the Mars mission? All the clues are here. Turn to page 77 for the solution.

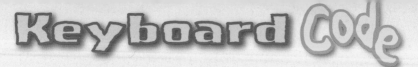

Keyboard Code

Commander Ripley has given Max and his team another challenge.
Use a computer keyboard to decode her mysterious message.

Hint: Replace each letter with one that's either to the left or the right of it on the keyboard.

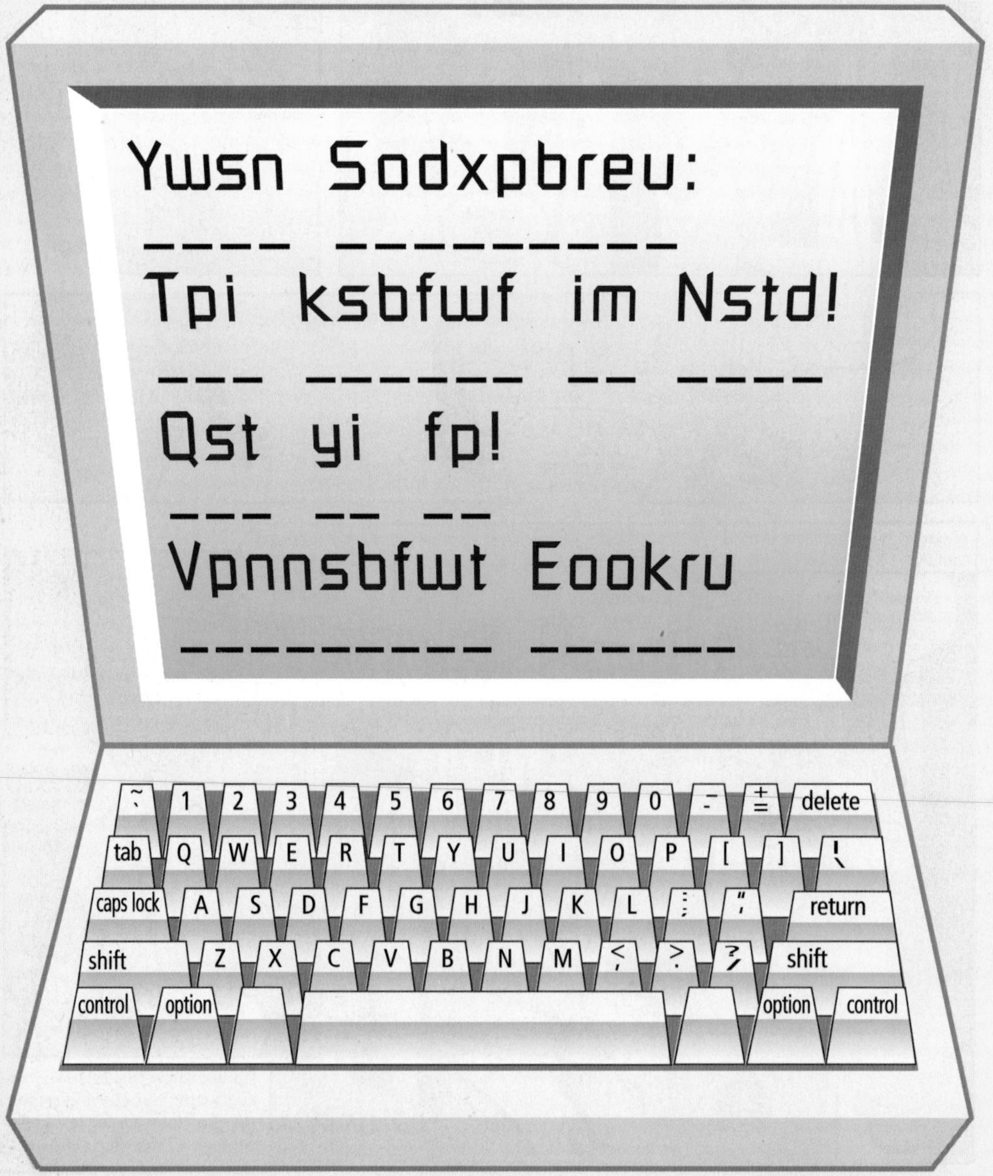
Ywsn Sodxpbreu:
____ __________
Tpi ksbfwf im Nstd!
___ ______ __ ____
Qst yi fp!
___ __ __
Vpnnsbfwt Eookru
__________ ______
~ 1 2 3 4 5 6 7 8 9 0 - + delete
tab Q W E R T Y U I O P [ ] \
caps lock A S D F G H J K L ; " return
shift Z X C V B N M < > ? shift
control option option control

ANSWER PAGE 84

The Case of the...

Ice Village Vandal

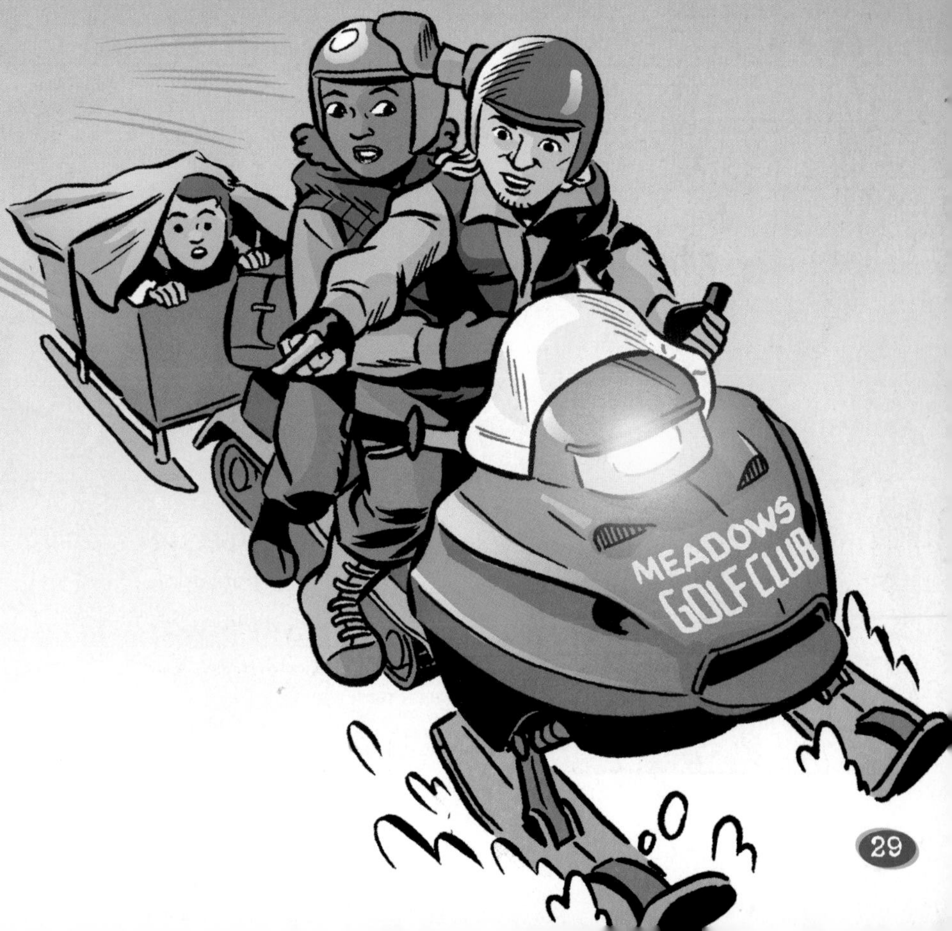
MEADOWS
GOLF CLUB

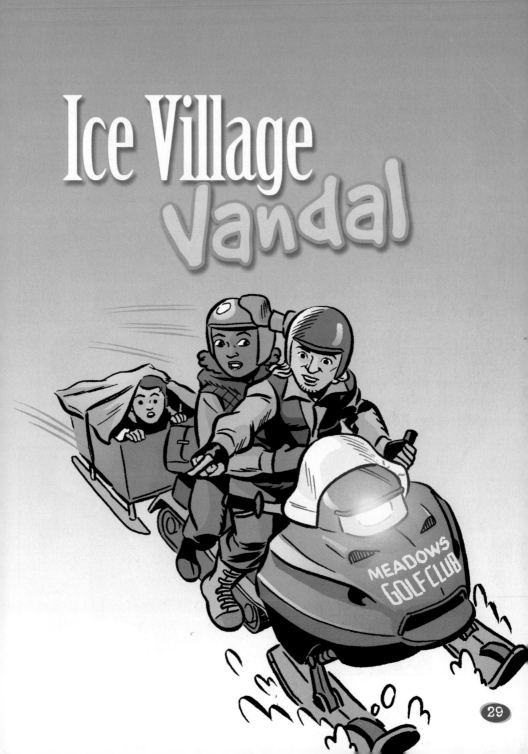

The Case of the Ice Village Vandal

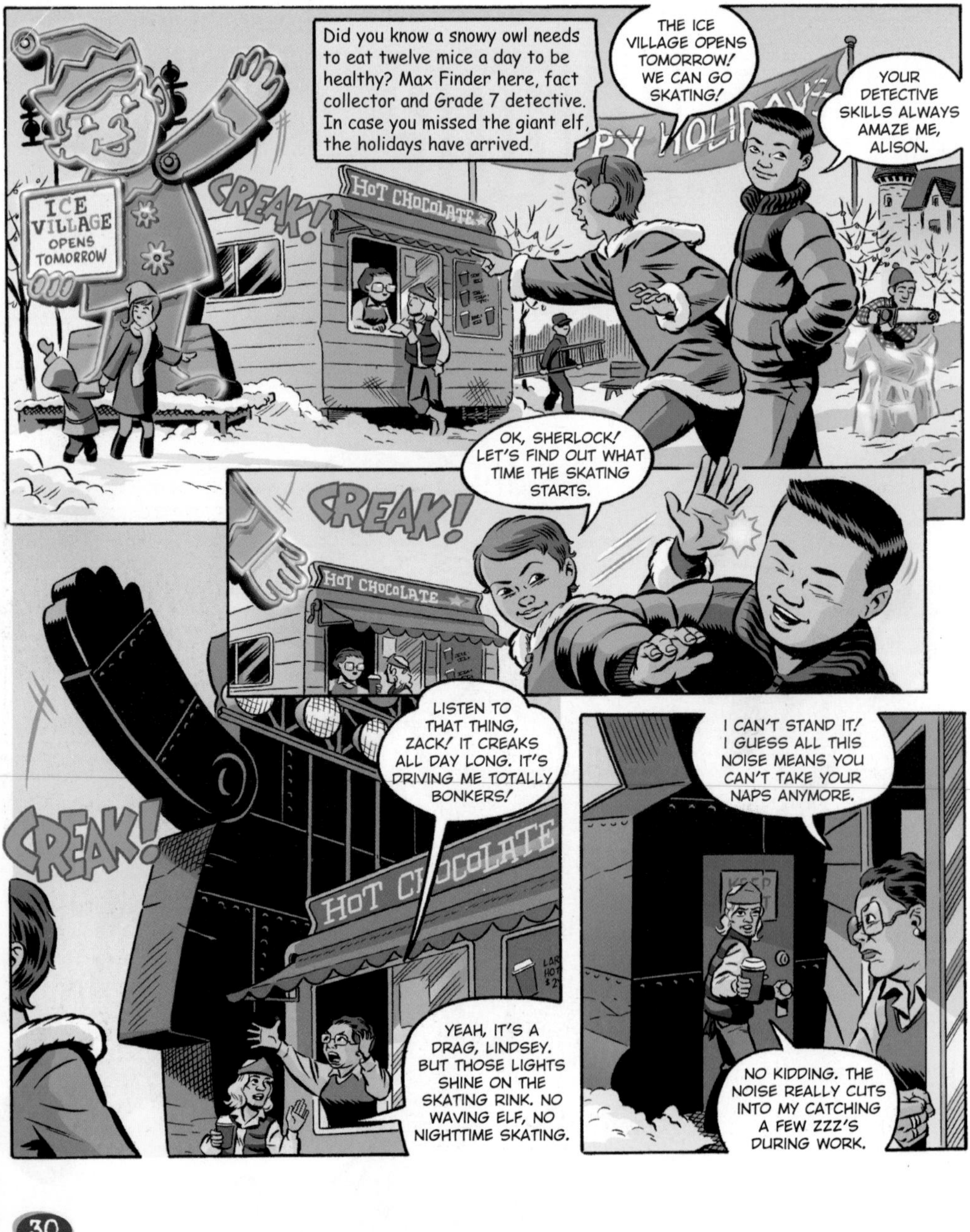

Did you know a snowy owl needs to eat twelve mice a day to be healthy? Max Finder here, fact collector and Grade 7 detective. In case you missed the giant elf, the holidays have arrived.
THE ICE VILLAGE OPENS TOMORROW! WE CAN GO SKATING!
YOUR DETECTIVE SKILLS ALWAYS AMAZE ME, ALISON.
ICE VILLAGE OPENS TOMORROW
HOT CHOCOLATE
CREAK!
OK, SHERLOCK! LET'S FIND OUT WHAT TIME THE SKATING STARTS.
CREAK!
HOT CHOCOLATE
LISTEN TO THAT THING, ZACK! IT CREAKS ALL DAY LONG. IT'S DRIVING ME TOTALLY BONKERS!
CREAK!
HOT CHOCOLATE
YEAH, IT'S A DRAG, LINDSEY. BUT THOSE LIGHTS SHINE ON THE SKATING RINK. NO WAVING ELF, NO NIGHTTIME SKATING.
I CAN'T STAND IT! I GUESS ALL THIS NOISE MEANS YOU CAN'T TAKE YOUR NAPS ANYMORE.
NO KIDDING. THE NOISE REALLY CUTS INTO MY CATCHING A FEW ZZZ'S DURING WORK.

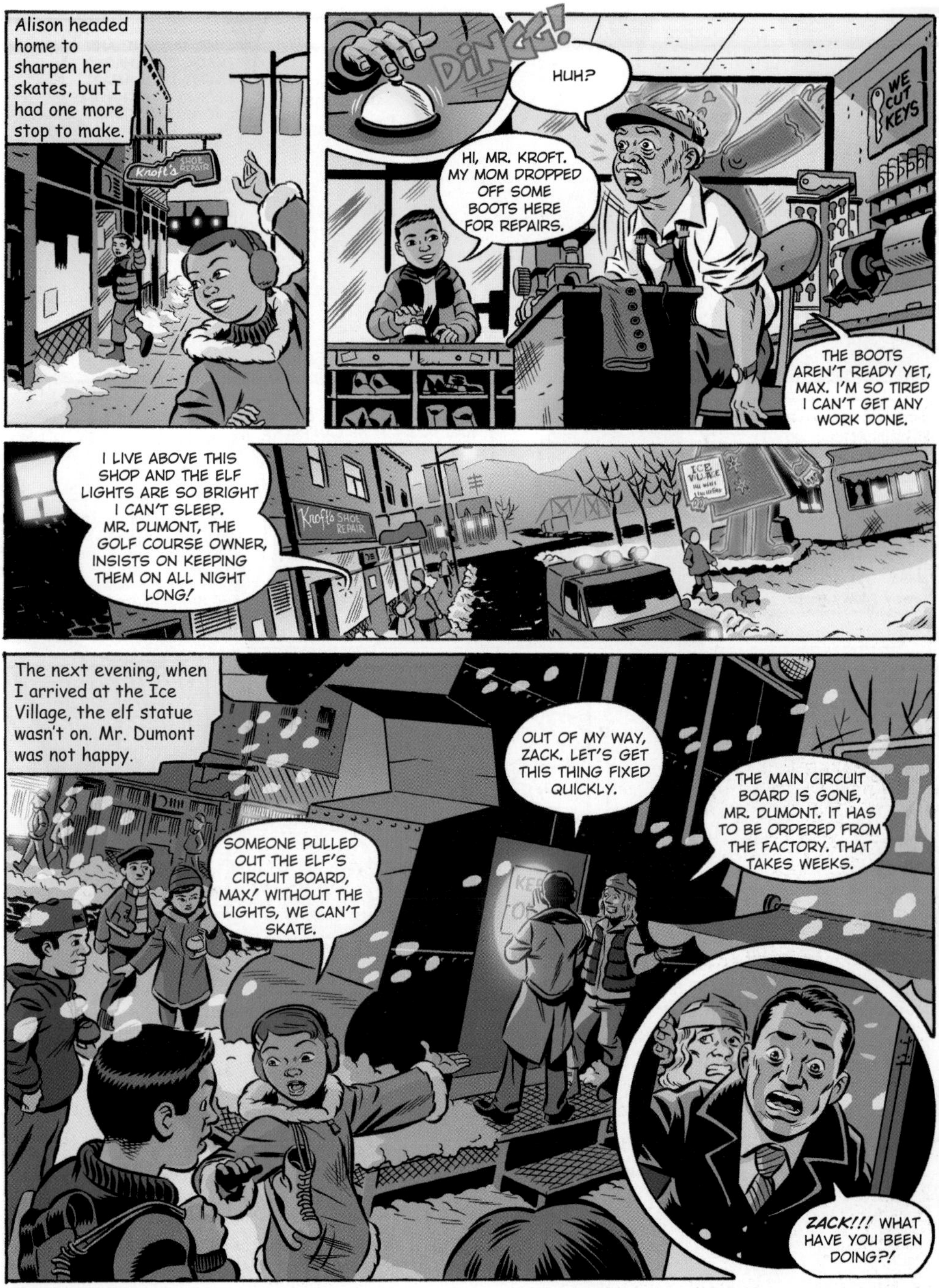
Alison headed home to sharpen her skates, but I had one more stop to make.
Kroft's SHOE REPAIR
DINGG!
HUH?
WE CUT KEYS
HI, MR. KROFT. MY MOM DROPPED OFF SOME BOOTS HERE FOR REPAIRS.
THE BOOTS AREN'T READY YET, MAX. I'M SO TIRED I CAN'T GET ANY WORK DONE.
I LIVE ABOVE THIS SHOP AND THE ELF LIGHTS ARE SO BRIGHT I CAN'T SLEEP. MR. DUMONT, THE GOLF COURSE OWNER, INSISTS ON KEEPING THEM ON ALL NIGHT LONG!
Kroft's SHOE REPAIR
The next evening, when I arrived at the Ice Village, the elf statue wasn't on. Mr. Dumont was not happy.
OUT OF MY WAY, ZACK. LET'S GET THIS THING FIXED QUICKLY.
THE MAIN CIRCUIT BOARD IS GONE, MR. DUMONT. IT HAS TO BE ORDERED FROM THE FACTORY. THAT TAKES WEEKS.
SOMEONE PULLED OUT THE ELF'S CIRCUIT BOARD, MAX! WITHOUT THE LIGHTS, WE CAN'T SKATE.
ZACK!!! WHAT HAVE YOU BEEN DOING?!

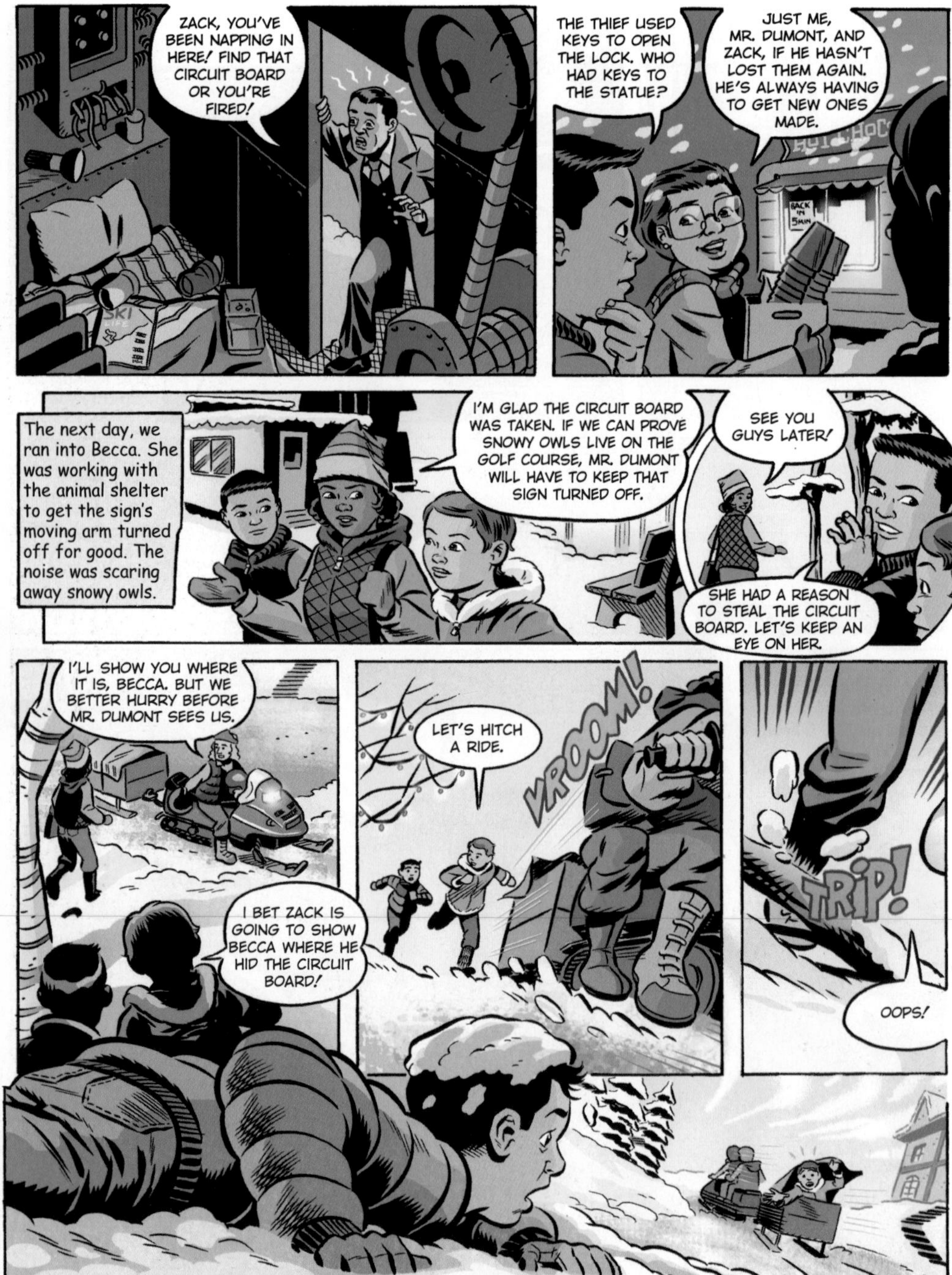

ZACK, YOU'VE BEEN NAPPING IN HERE! FIND THAT CIRCUIT BOARD OR YOU'RE FIRED!
THE THIEF USED KEYS TO OPEN THE LOCK. WHO HAD KEYS TO THE STATUE?
JUST ME, MR. DUMONT, AND ZACK, IF HE HASN'T LOST THEM AGAIN. HE'S ALWAYS HAVING TO GET NEW ONES MADE.
BACK IN 5MIN
The next day, we ran into Becca. She was working with the animal shelter to get the sign's moving arm turned off for good. The noise was scaring away snowy owls.
I'M GLAD THE CIRCUIT BOARD WAS TAKEN. IF WE CAN PROVE SNOWY OWLS LIVE ON THE GOLF COURSE, MR. DUMONT WILL HAVE TO KEEP THAT SIGN TURNED OFF.
SEE YOU GUYS LATER!
SHE HAD A REASON TO STEAL THE CIRCUIT BOARD. LET'S KEEP AN EYE ON HER.
I'LL SHOW YOU WHERE IT IS, BECCA. BUT WE BETTER HURRY BEFORE MR. DUMONT SEES US.
I BET ZACK IS GOING TO SHOW BECCA WHERE HE HID THE CIRCUIT BOARD!
LET'S HITCH A RIDE.
VROOOM!
TRIP!
OOPS!

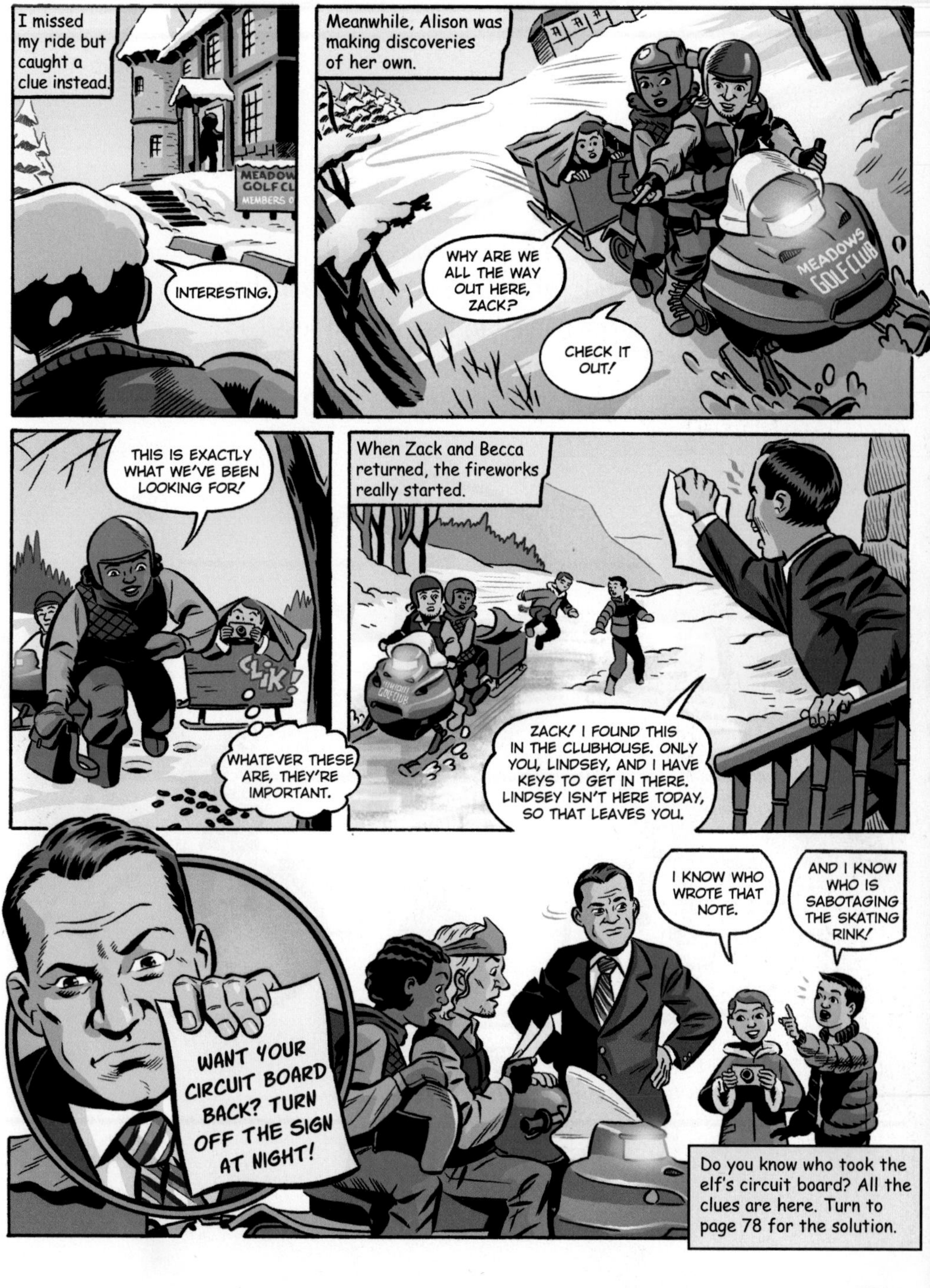
I missed my ride but caught a clue instead.
MEADOWS GOLF CLU
MEMBERS O
INTERESTING.
Meanwhile, Alison was making discoveries of her own.
MEADOWS GOLF CLUB
WHY ARE WE ALL THE WAY OUT HERE, ZACK?
CHECK IT OUT!
THIS IS EXACTLY WHAT WE'VE BEEN LOOKING FOR!
CLIK!
WHATEVER THESE ARE, THEY'RE IMPORTANT.
When Zack and Becca returned, the fireworks really started.
ZACK! I FOUND THIS IN THE CLUBHOUSE. ONLY YOU, LINDSEY, AND I HAVE KEYS TO GET IN THERE. LINDSEY ISN'T HERE TODAY, SO THAT LEAVES YOU.
WANT YOUR CIRCUIT BOARD BACK? TURN OFF THE SIGN AT NIGHT!
I KNOW WHO WROTE THAT NOTE.
AND I KNOW WHO IS SABOTAGING THE SKATING RINK!
Do you know who took the elf's circuit board? All the clues are here. Turn to page 78 for the solution.

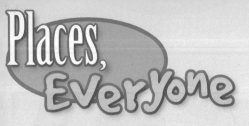

Places, Everyone

Max and Alison play hockey on Saturdays with their friends.

Figure out which kid played in each position on Max's team.

Players:
Max, Alison, Basher, Jessica, Ethan, and Becca.

Clues:

1. The goalie was a girl.
2. Both kids who played defence were boys.
3. Becca played to the right of Jessica.
4. Basher was left wing.
5. Max played directly behind Becca.

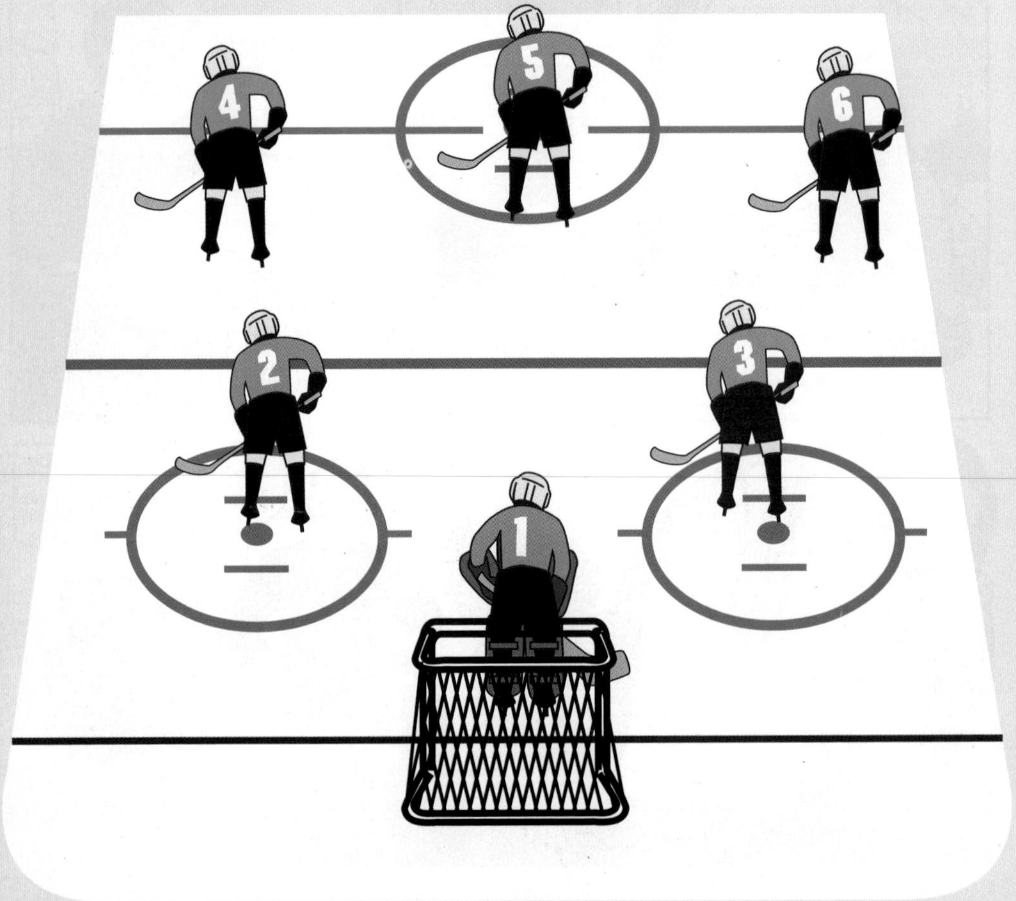

4
5
6
2
3
1

ANSWER PAGE 84

CAST-OFF Costume

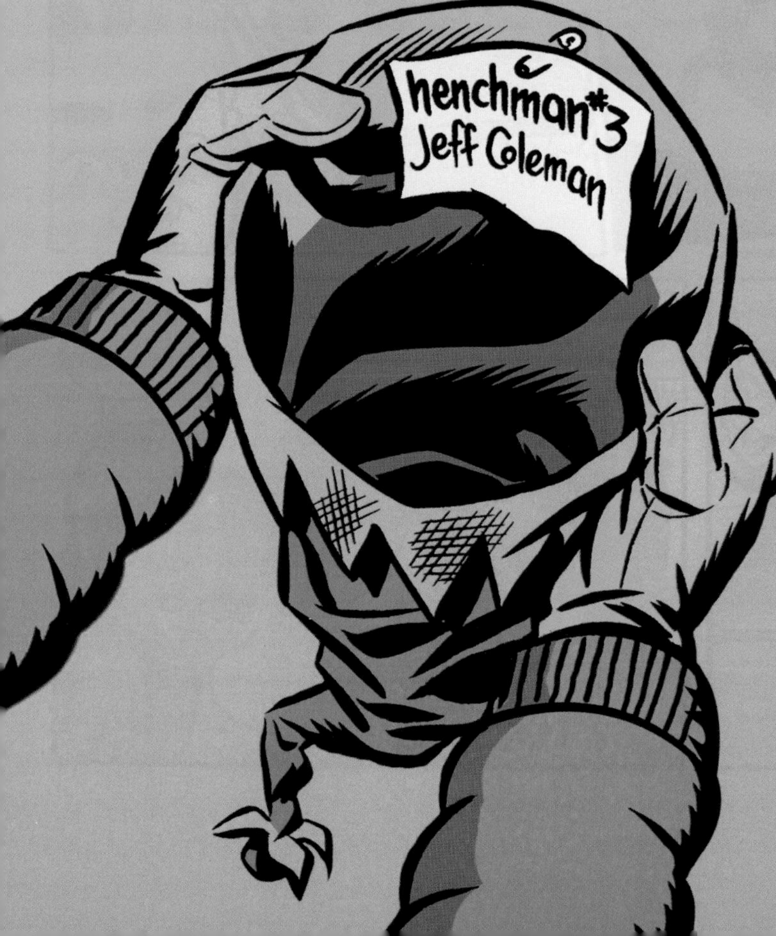
henchman#3
Jeff Coleman

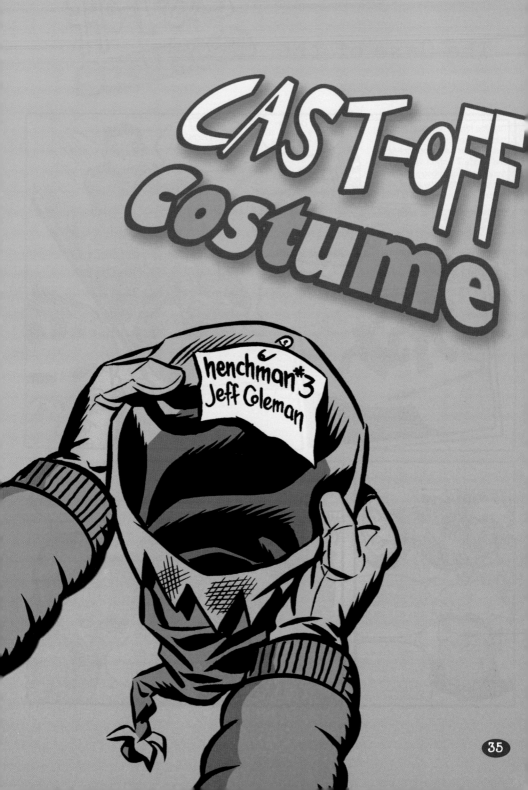

The Case of the CAST-OFF Costume

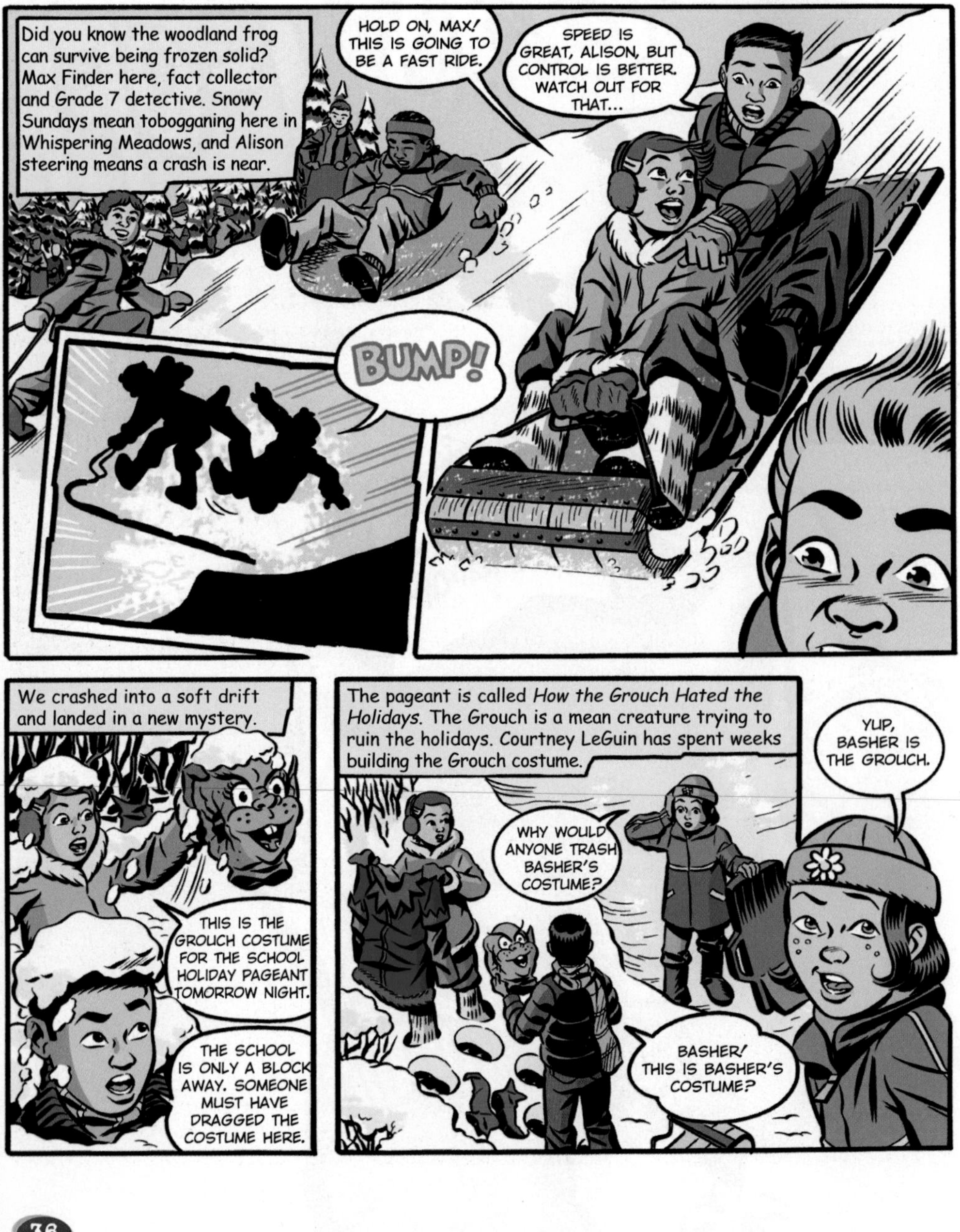

Did you know the woodland frog can survive being frozen solid? Max Finder here, fact collector and Grade 7 detective. Snowy Sundays mean tobogganing here in Whispering Meadows, and Alison steering means a crash is near.
HOLD ON, MAX! THIS IS GOING TO BE A FAST RIDE.
SPEED IS GREAT, ALISON, BUT CONTROL IS BETTER. WATCH OUT FOR THAT...
BUMP!
We crashed into a soft drift and landed in a new mystery.
THIS IS THE GROUCH COSTUME FOR THE SCHOOL HOLIDAY PAGEANT TOMORROW NIGHT.
THE SCHOOL IS ONLY A BLOCK AWAY. SOMEONE MUST HAVE DRAGGED THE COSTUME HERE.
The pageant is called *How the Grouch Hated the Holidays*. The Grouch is a mean creature trying to ruin the holidays. Courtney LeGuin has spent weeks building the Grouch costume.
YUP, BASHER IS THE GROUCH.
WHY WOULD ANYONE TRASH BASHER'S COSTUME?
BASHER! THIS IS BASHER'S COSTUME?

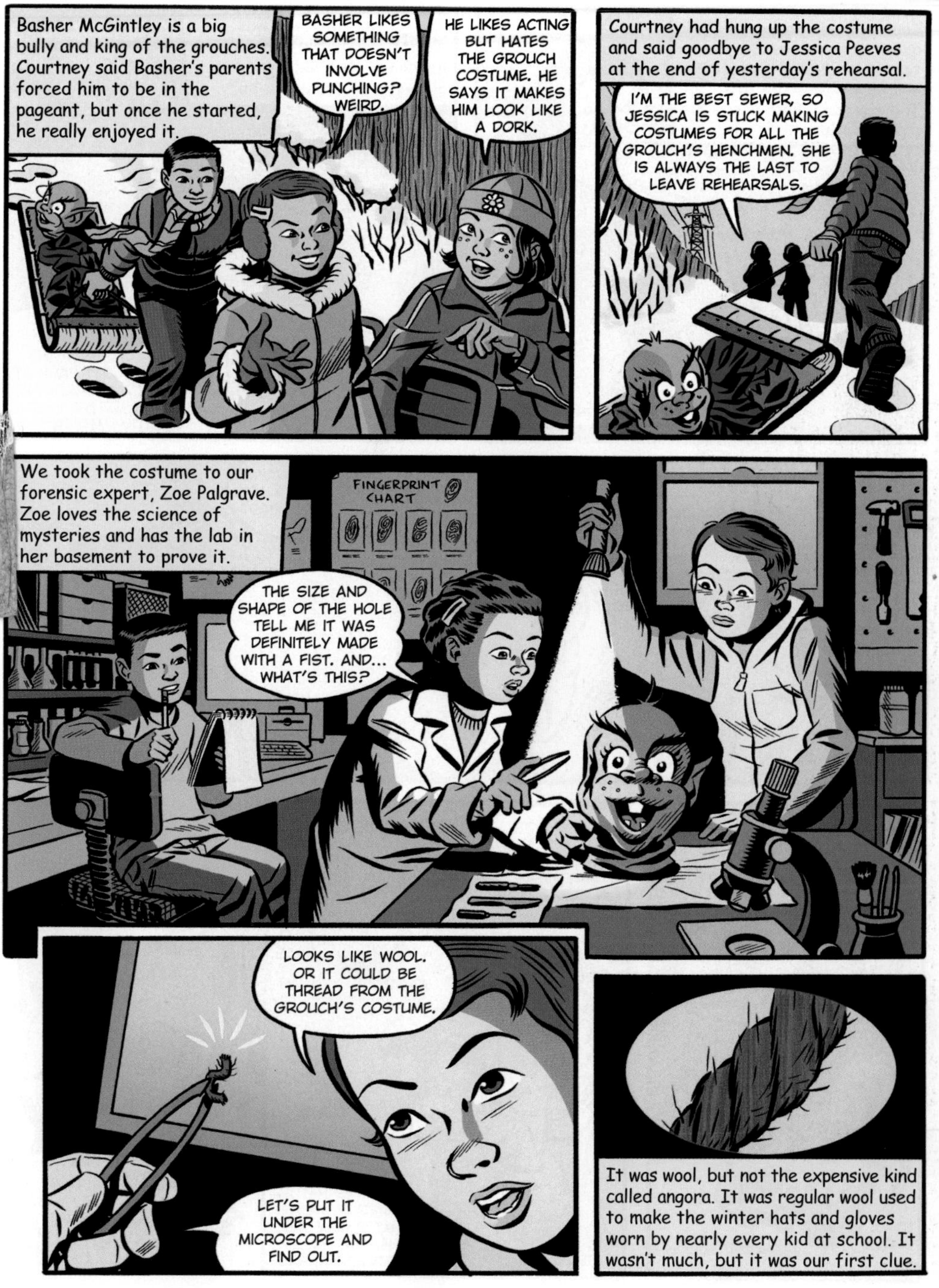
Basher McGintley is a big bully and king of the grouches. Courtney said Basher's parents forced him to be in the pageant, but once he started, he really enjoyed it.
BASHER LIKES SOMETHING THAT DOESN'T INVOLVE PUNCHING? WEIRD.
HE LIKES ACTING BUT HATES THE GROUCH COSTUME. HE SAYS IT MAKES HIM LOOK LIKE A DORK.
Courtney had hung up the costume and said goodbye to Jessica Peeves at the end of yesterday's rehearsal.
I'M THE BEST SEWER, SO JESSICA IS STUCK MAKING COSTUMES FOR ALL THE GROUCH'S HENCHMEN. SHE IS ALWAYS THE LAST TO LEAVE REHEARSALS.
We took the costume to our forensic expert, Zoe Palgrave. Zoe loves the science of mysteries and has the lab in her basement to prove it.
FINGERPRINT CHART
THE SIZE AND SHAPE OF THE HOLE TELL ME IT WAS DEFINITELY MADE WITH A FIST. AND... WHAT'S THIS?
LOOKS LIKE WOOL. OR IT COULD BE THREAD FROM THE GROUCH'S COSTUME.
LET'S PUT IT UNDER THE MICROSCOPE AND FIND OUT.
It was wool, but not the expensive kind called angora. It was regular wool used to make the winter hats and gloves worn by nearly every kid at school. It wasn't much, but it was our first clue.

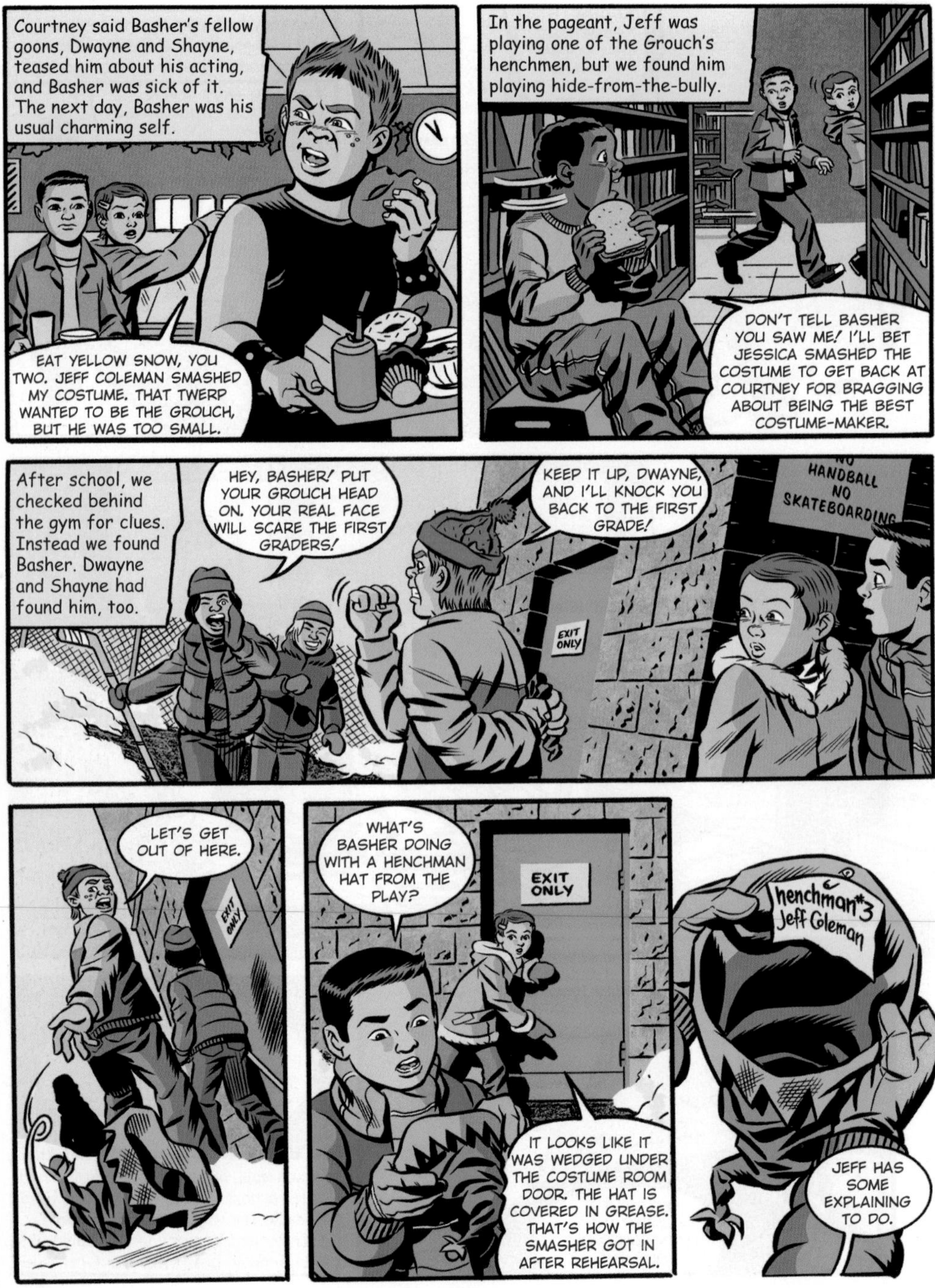

Courtney said Basher's fellow goons, Dwayne and Shayne, teased him about his acting, and Basher was sick of it. The next day, Basher was his usual charming self.
EAT YELLOW SNOW, YOU TWO. JEFF COLEMAN SMASHED MY COSTUME. THAT TWERP WANTED TO BE THE GROUCH, BUT HE WAS TOO SMALL.
In the pageant, Jeff was playing one of the Grouch's henchmen, but we found him playing hide-from-the-bully.
DON'T TELL BASHER YOU SAW ME! I'LL BET JESSICA SMASHED THE COSTUME TO GET BACK AT COURTNEY FOR BRAGGING ABOUT BEING THE BEST COSTUME-MAKER.
After school, we checked behind the gym for clues. Instead we found Basher. Dwayne and Shayne had found him, too.
HEY, BASHER! PUT YOUR GROUCH HEAD ON. YOUR REAL FACE WILL SCARE THE FIRST GRADERS!
KEEP IT UP, DWAYNE, AND I'LL KNOCK YOU BACK TO THE FIRST GRADE!
HANDBALL NO SKATEBOARDING
EXIT ONLY
LET'S GET OUT OF HERE.
EXIT ONLY
WHAT'S BASHER DOING WITH A HENCHMAN HAT FROM THE PLAY?
EXIT ONLY
IT LOOKS LIKE IT WAS WEDGED UNDER THE COSTUME ROOM DOOR. THE HAT IS COVERED IN GREASE. THAT'S HOW THE SMASHER GOT IN AFTER REHEARSAL.
henchman #3 Jeff Coleman
JEFF HAS SOME EXPLAINING TO DO.

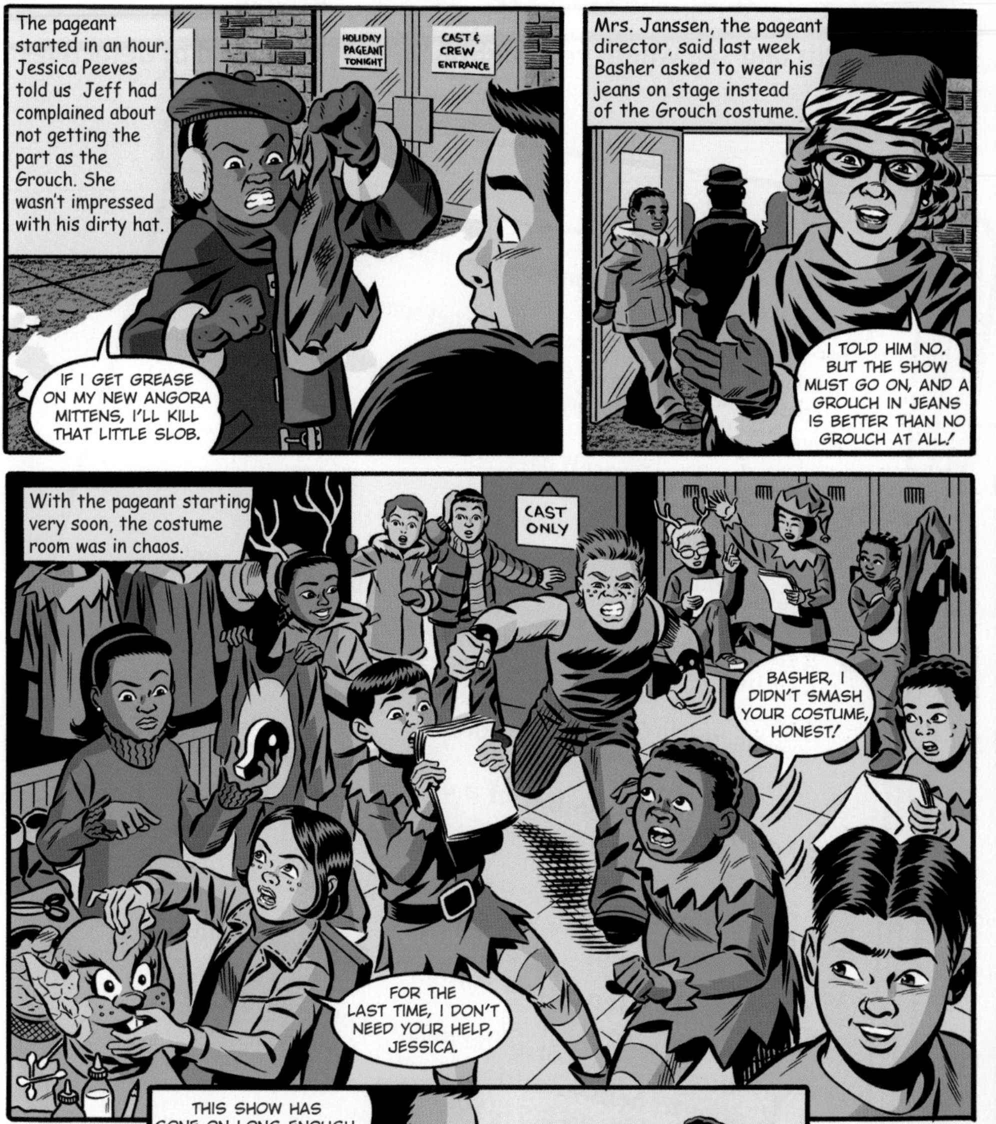
The pageant started in an hour. Jessica Peeves told us Jeff had complained about not getting the part as the Grouch. She wasn't impressed with his dirty hat.
HOLIDAY PAGEANT TONIGHT
CAST & CREW ENTRANCE
IF I GET GREASE ON MY NEW ANGORA MITTENS, I'LL KILL THAT LITTLE SLOB.
Mrs. Janssen, the pageant director, said last week Basher asked to wear his jeans on stage instead of the Grouch costume.
I TOLD HIM NO. BUT THE SHOW MUST GO ON, AND A GROUCH IN JEANS IS BETTER THAN NO GROUCH AT ALL!
With the pageant starting very soon, the costume room was in chaos.
CAST ONLY
BASHER, I DIDN'T SMASH YOUR COSTUME, HONEST!
FOR THE LAST TIME, I DON'T NEED YOUR HELP, JESSICA.

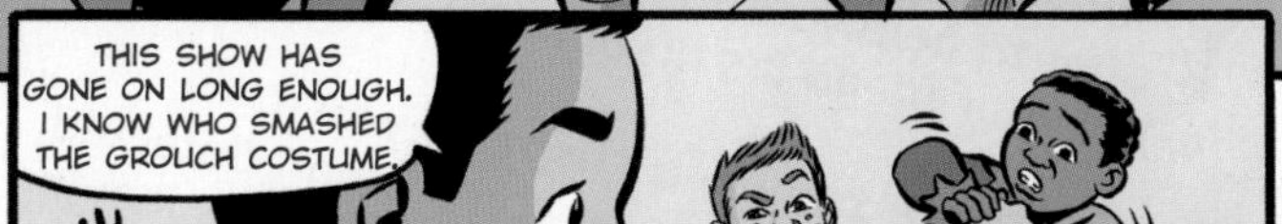
THIS SHOW HAS GONE ON LONG ENOUGH. I KNOW WHO SMASHED THE GROUCH COSTUME.

Do you know who wrecked the Grouch costume? All the clues are here. Turn to page 78 for the solution.

WHAT KIND OF DETECTIVE WOULD YOU BE?

Take this quiz and see where you might belong in the world of detectives.

1. **Your sister's diary has gone missing and she asks for help. You:**
   a. interview everyone in the house to get some clues
   b. search her bedroom for evidence
   c. put the diary back before she catches you with it

2. **You'd describe yourself as:**
   a. mischievous
   b. born with an eye for detail
   c. suspicious

3. **A famous painting was stolen from a museum. If you had been first on the scene, you would have:**
   a. asked to examine the videotapes that captured the robbery
   b. collected fingerprints and other clues from the museum
   c. left it up to the police to solve

4. **If you were a member of a crime team like the ones on TV's C.S.I. you'd be:**
   a. the detective who interviews the suspects
   b. the crime scene investigator
   c. the police officer who secures the scene

5. **Your best friend says someone has been rummaging through his locker. You:**
   a. secretly try to solve the mystery on your own
   b. offer to help your friend search for clues
   c. tell your friend it's no big deal since nothing's missing

6. **If you were tailing a suspect, you'd:**
   a. keep a safe distance so you weren't detected
   b. try to gather evidence the suspect was leaving behind
   c. call for back-up

40

RATINGS PAGE 84

The Case of the...

Slime Tank Sabotage

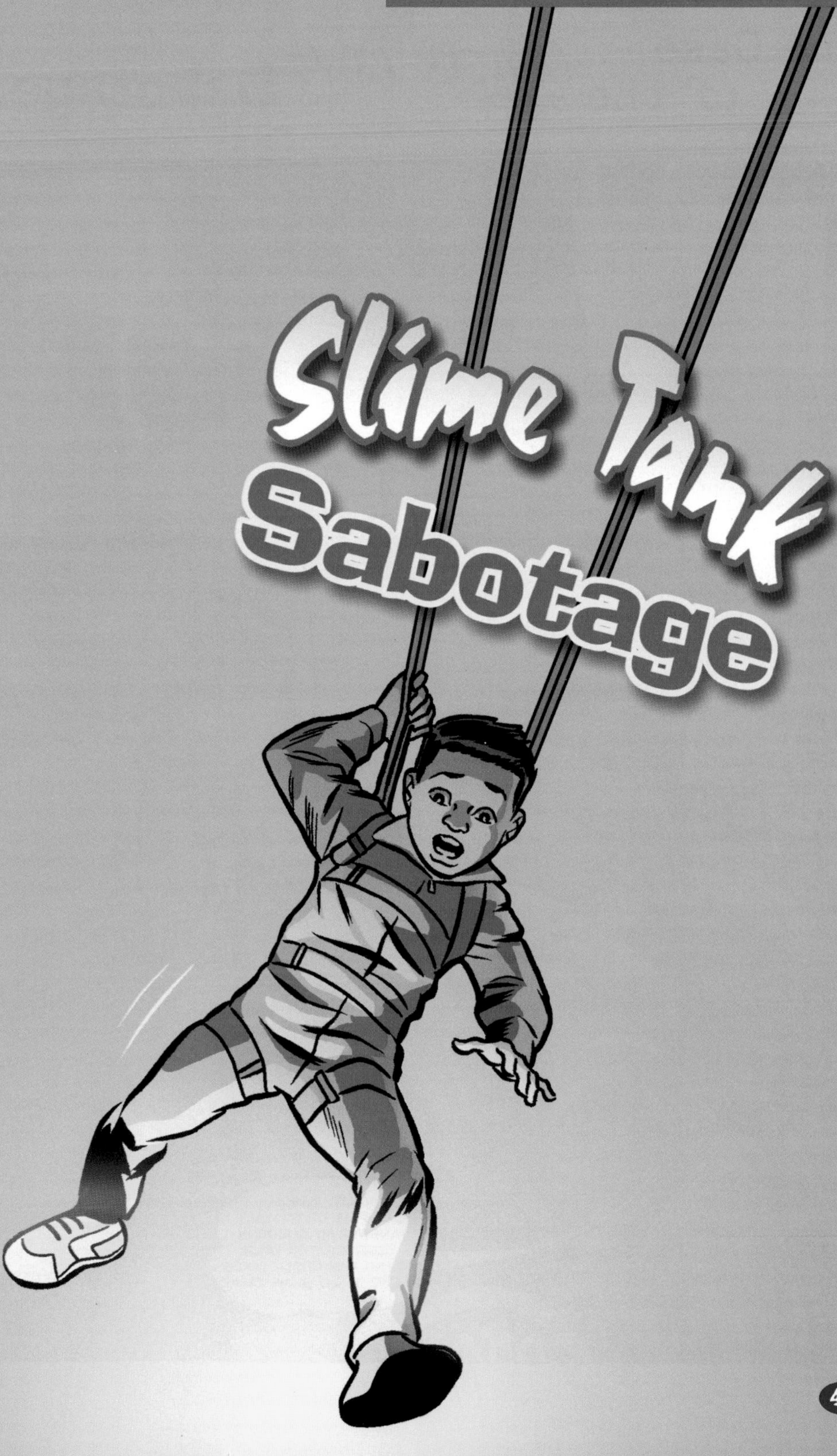

The Case of the Slime Tank Sabotage

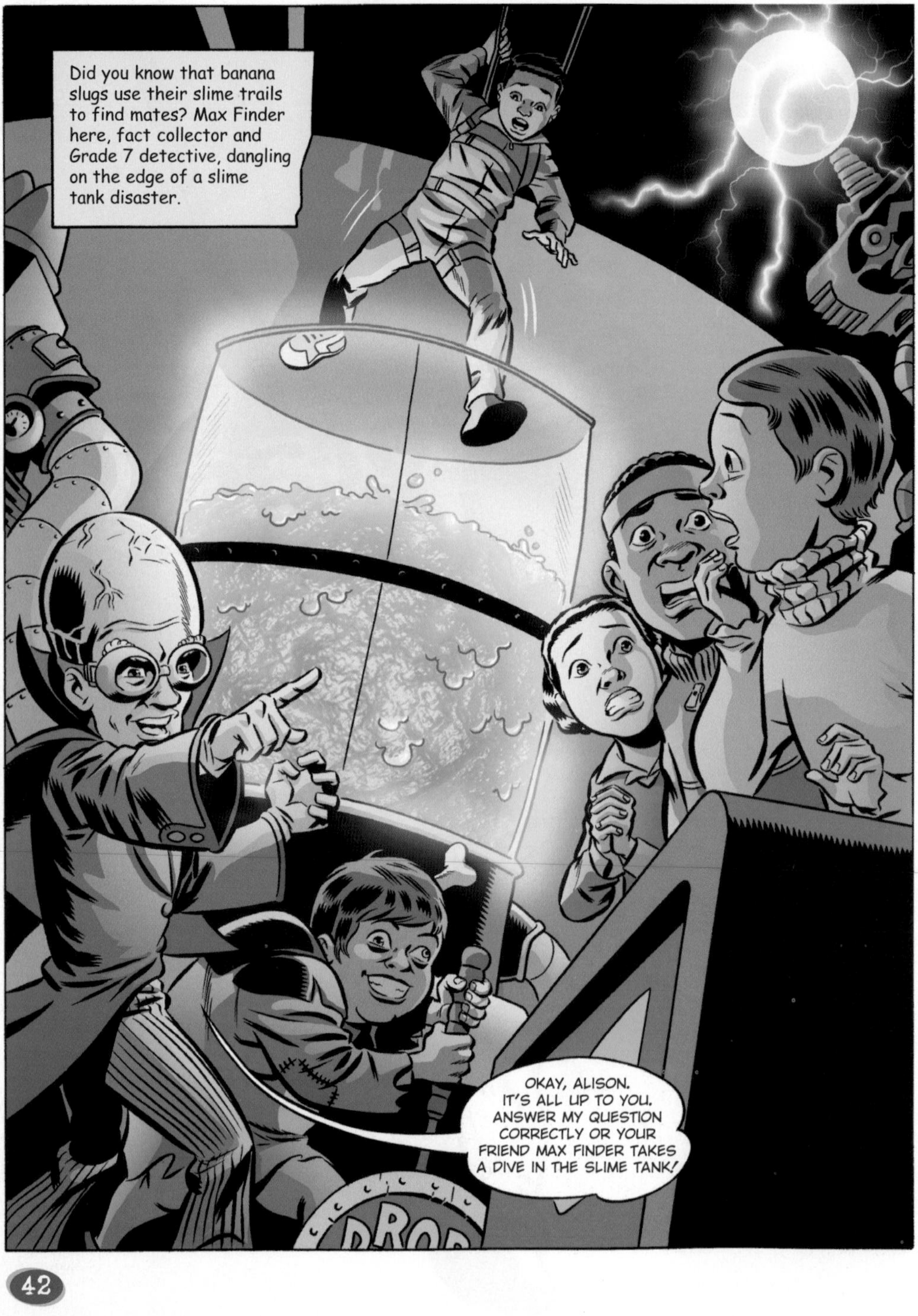
Did you know that banana slugs use their slime trails to find mates? Max Finder here, fact collector and Grade 7 detective, dangling on the edge of a slime tank disaster.
OKAY, ALISON. IT'S ALL UP TO YOU. ANSWER MY QUESTION CORRECTLY OR YOUR FRIEND MAX FINDER TAKES A DIVE IN THE SLIME TANK!

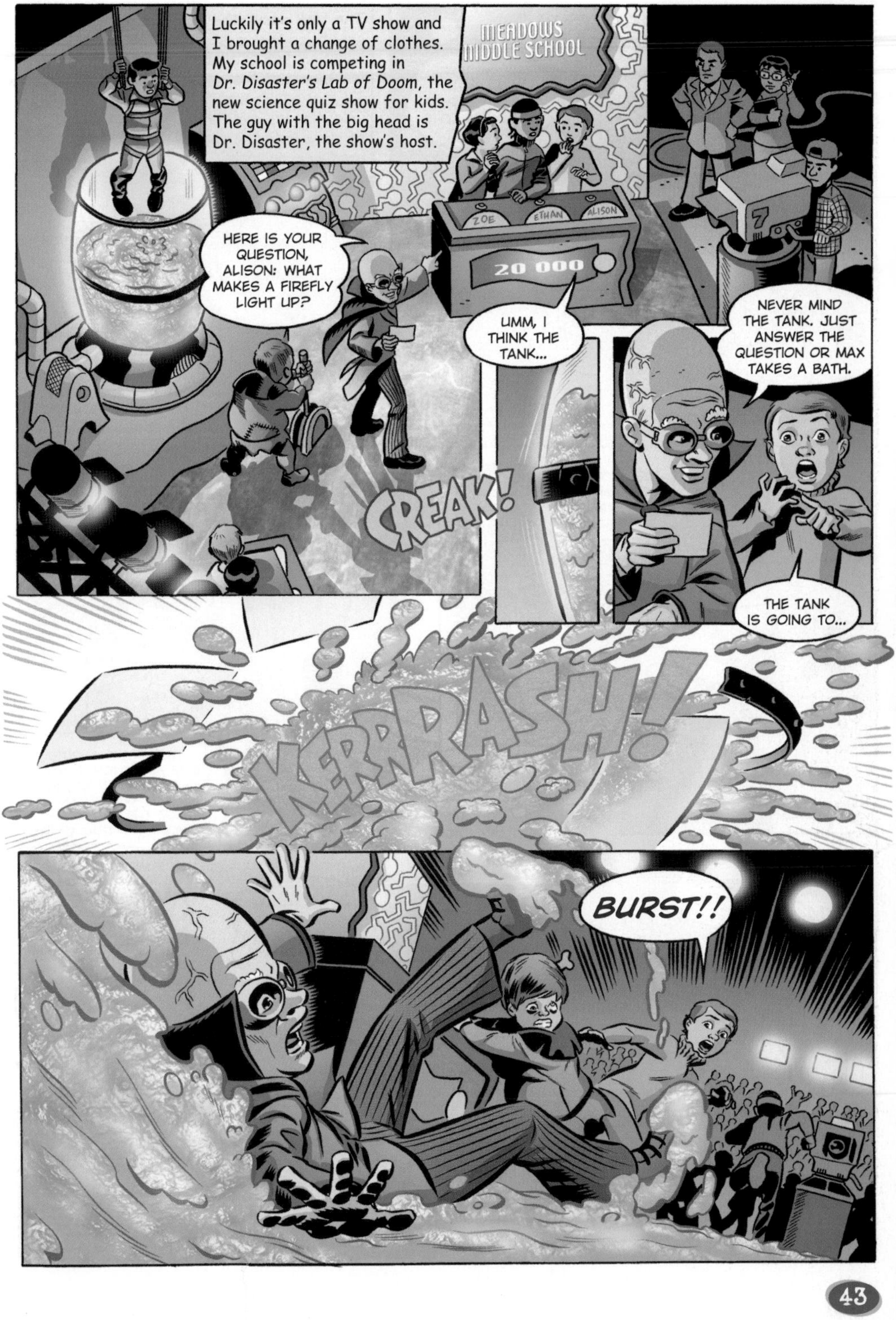
Luckily it's only a TV show and I brought a change of clothes. My school is competing in *Dr. Disaster's Lab of Doom*, the new science quiz show for kids. The guy with the big head is Dr. Disaster, the show's host.
MEADOWS MIDDLE SCHOOL
ZOE
ETHAN
ALISON
20 000
HERE IS YOUR QUESTION, ALISON: WHAT MAKES A FIREFLY LIGHT UP?
UMM, I THINK THE TANK...
CREAK!
NEVER MIND THE TANK. JUST ANSWER THE QUESTION OR MAX TAKES A BATH.
THE TANK IS GOING TO...
KERRRASH!
BURST!!

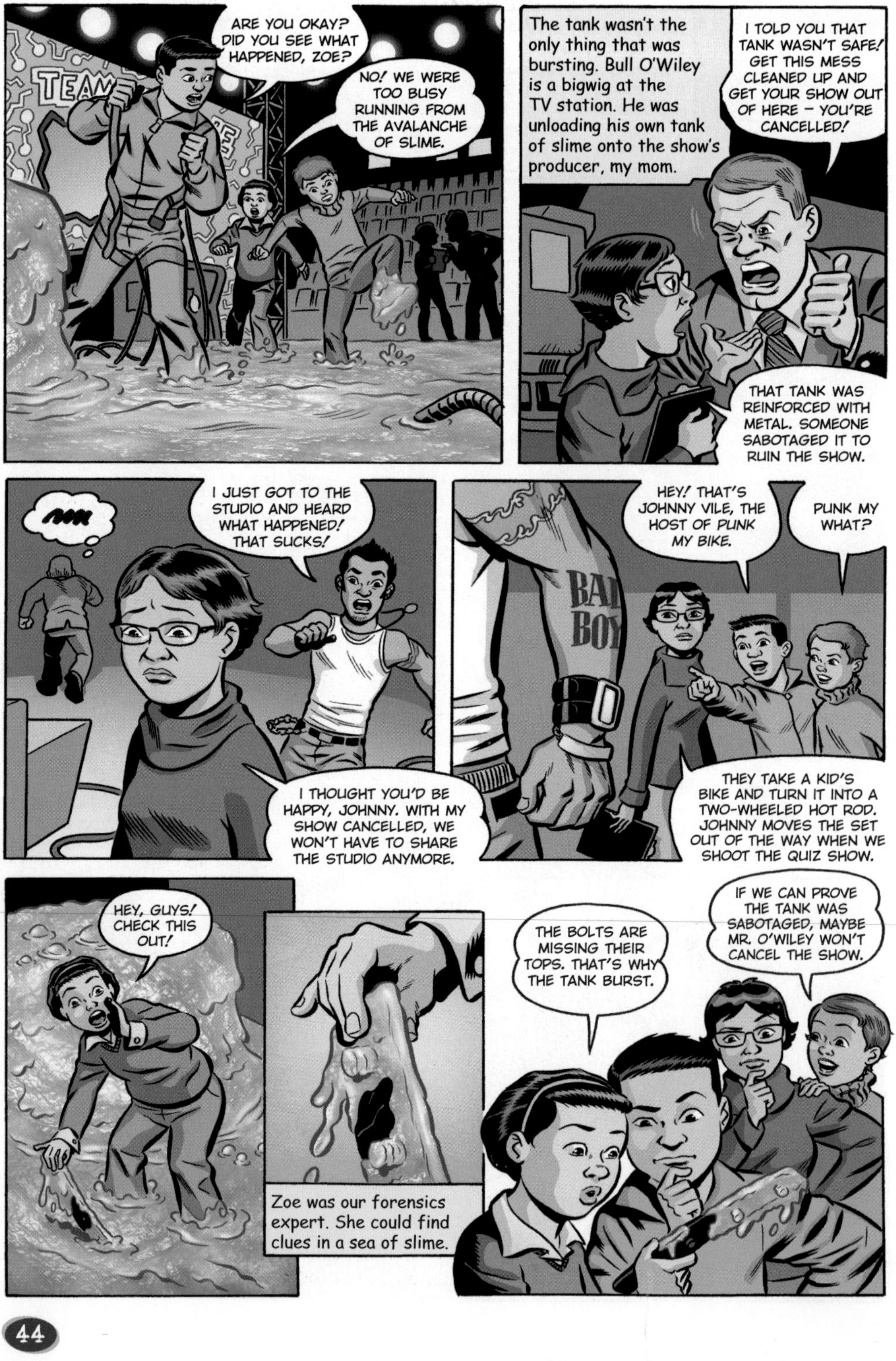
ARE YOU OKAY? DID YOU SEE WHAT HAPPENED, ZOE?
NO! WE WERE TOO BUSY RUNNING FROM THE AVALANCHE OF SLIME.
The tank wasn't the only thing that was bursting. Bull O'Wiley is a bigwig at the TV station. He was unloading his own tank of slime onto the show's producer, my mom.
I TOLD YOU THAT TANK WASN'T SAFE! GET THIS MESS CLEANED UP AND GET YOUR SHOW OUT OF HERE – YOU'RE CANCELLED!
THAT TANK WAS REINFORCED WITH METAL. SOMEONE SABOTAGED IT TO RUIN THE SHOW.
I JUST GOT TO THE STUDIO AND HEARD WHAT HAPPENED! THAT SUCKS!
I THOUGHT YOU'D BE HAPPY, JOHNNY. WITH MY SHOW CANCELLED, WE WON'T HAVE TO SHARE THE STUDIO ANYMORE.
HEY! THAT'S JOHNNY VILE, THE HOST OF PUNK MY BIKE.
PUNK MY WHAT?
BAD BOY
THEY TAKE A KID'S BIKE AND TURN IT INTO A TWO-WHEELED HOT ROD. JOHNNY MOVES THE SET OUT OF THE WAY WHEN WE SHOOT THE QUIZ SHOW.
HEY, GUYS! CHECK THIS OUT!
Zoe was our forensics expert. She could find clues in a sea of slime.
THE BOLTS ARE MISSING THEIR TOPS. THAT'S WHY THE TANK BURST.
IF WE CAN PROVE THE TANK WAS SABOTAGED, MAYBE MR. O'WILEY WON'T CANCEL THE SHOW.

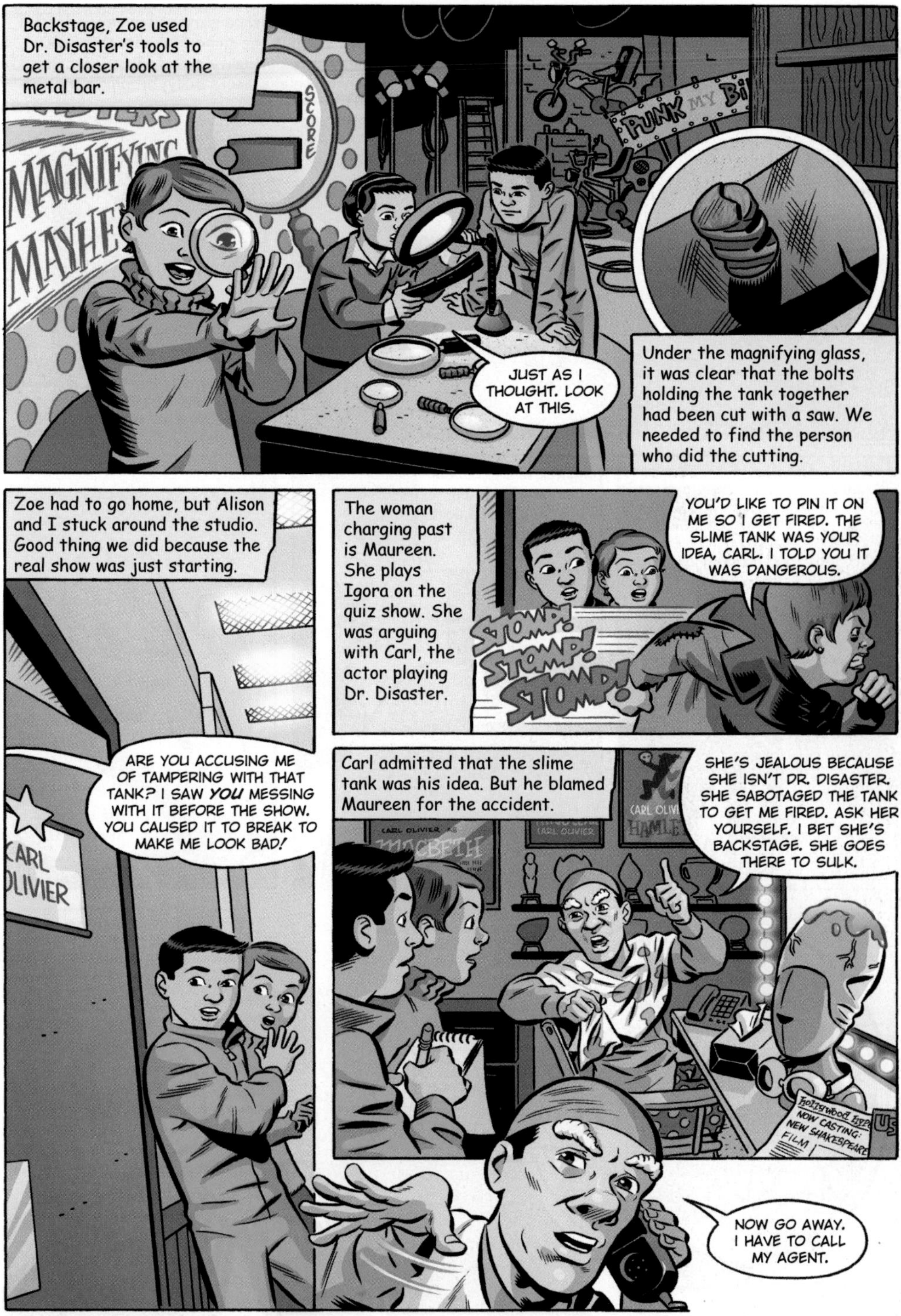

Backstage, Zoe used Dr. Disaster's tools to get a closer look at the metal bar.
MAGNIFYING MAYHE
SCORE
PUNK MY BI
JUST AS I THOUGHT. LOOK AT THIS.
Under the magnifying glass, it was clear that the bolts holding the tank together had been cut with a saw. We needed to find the person who did the cutting.
Zoe had to go home, but Alison and I stuck around the studio. Good thing we did because the real show was just starting.
The woman charging past is Maureen. She plays Igora on the quiz show. She was arguing with Carl, the actor playing Dr. Disaster.
YOU'D LIKE TO PIN IT ON ME SO I GET FIRED. THE SLIME TANK WAS YOUR IDEA, CARL. I TOLD YOU IT WAS DANGEROUS.
STOMP! STOMP! STOMP!
CARL OLIVIER
ARE YOU ACCUSING ME OF TAMPERING WITH THAT TANK? I SAW *YOU* MESSING WITH IT BEFORE THE SHOW. YOU CAUSED IT TO BREAK TO MAKE ME LOOK BAD!
Carl admitted that the slime tank was his idea. But he blamed Maureen for the accident.
CARL OLIVIER AS MACBETH
CARL OLIVIER
CARL OLIVIER HAMLET
SHE'S JEALOUS BECAUSE SHE ISN'T DR. DISASTER. SHE SABOTAGED THE TANK TO GET ME FIRED. ASK HER YOURSELF. I BET SHE'S BACKSTAGE. SHE GOES THERE TO SULK.
NOW CASTING: NEW SHAKESPEARE FILM
NOW GO AWAY. I HAVE TO CALL MY AGENT.

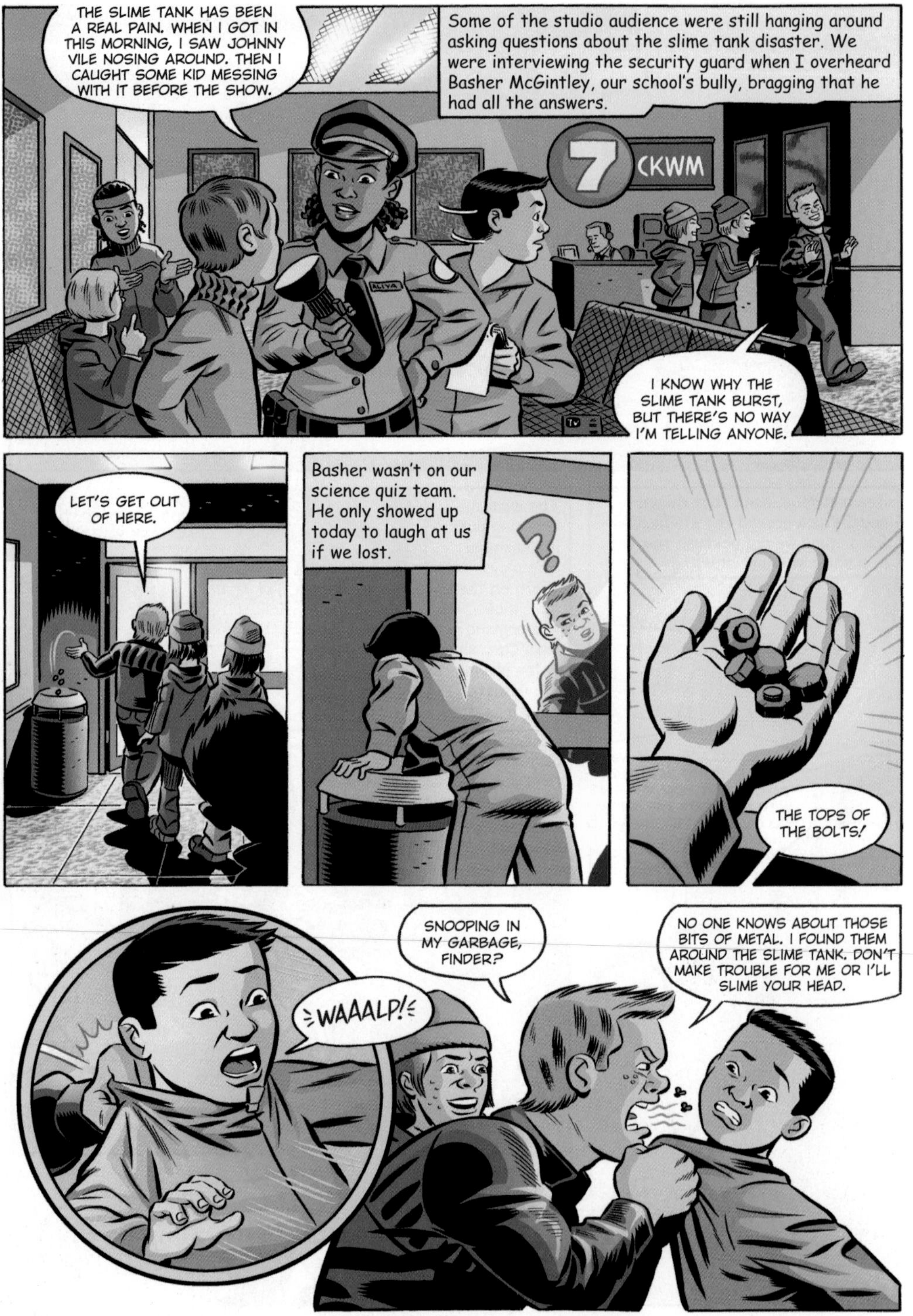
THE SLIME TANK HAS BEEN A REAL PAIN. WHEN I GOT IN THIS MORNING, I SAW JOHNNY VILE NOSING AROUND. THEN I CAUGHT SOME KID MESSING WITH IT BEFORE THE SHOW.
Some of the studio audience were still hanging around asking questions about the slime tank disaster. We were interviewing the security guard when I overheard Basher McGintley, our school's bully, bragging that he had all the answers.
7 CKWM
ALIYA
I KNOW WHY THE SLIME TANK BURST, BUT THERE'S NO WAY I'M TELLING ANYONE.
LET'S GET OUT OF HERE.
Basher wasn't on our science quiz team. He only showed up today to laugh at us if we lost.
?
THE TOPS OF THE BOLTS!
WAAALP!
SNOOPING IN MY GARBAGE, FINDER?
NO ONE KNOWS ABOUT THOSE BITS OF METAL. I FOUND THEM AROUND THE SLIME TANK. DON'T MAKE TROUBLE FOR ME OR I'LL SLIME YOUR HEAD.

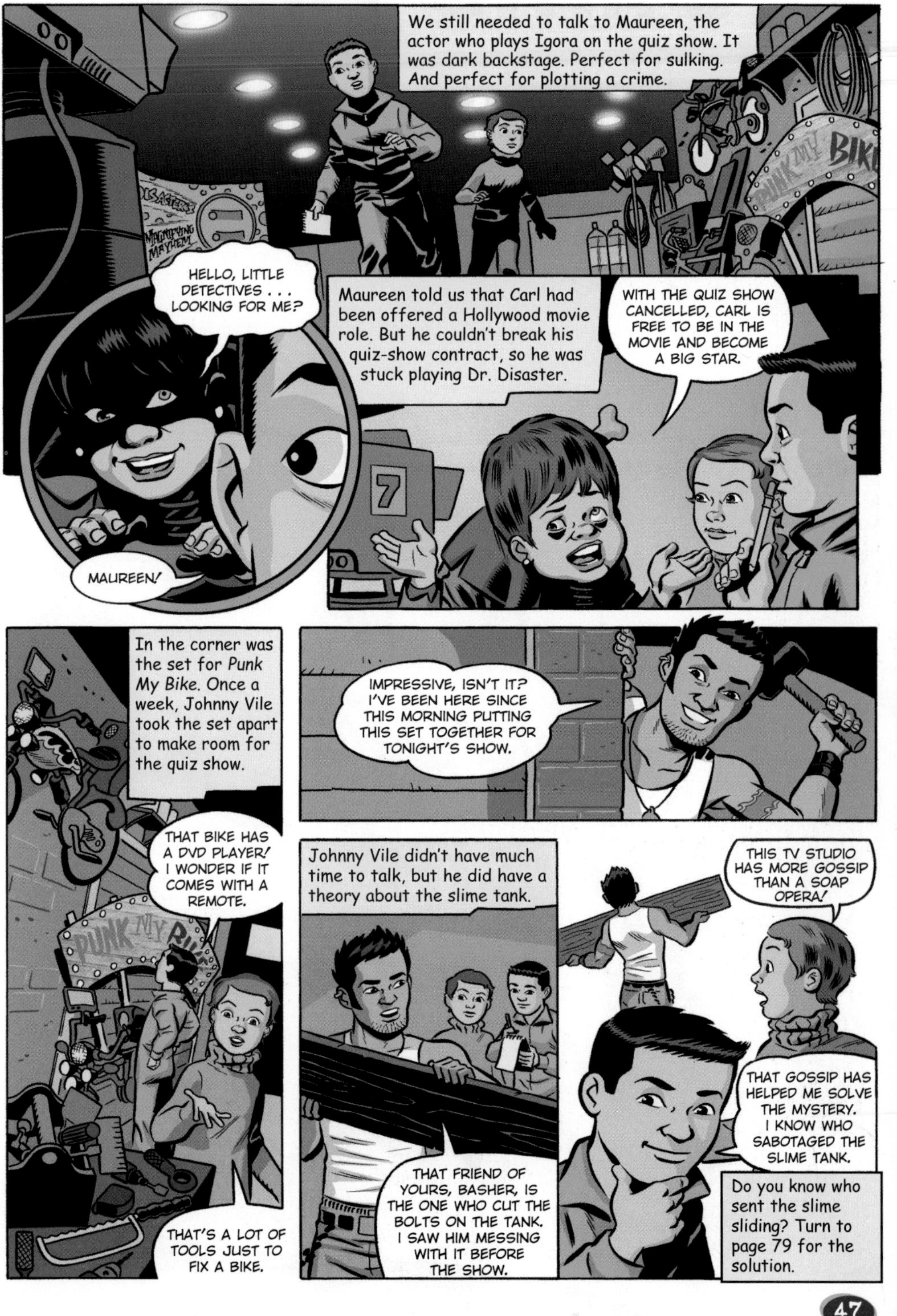
We still needed to talk to Maureen, the actor who plays Igora on the quiz show. It was dark backstage. Perfect for sulking. And perfect for plotting a crime.
PUNK MY BIKE
HELLO, LITTLE DETECTIVES . . . LOOKING FOR ME?
MAUREEN!
Maureen told us that Carl had been offered a Hollywood movie role. But he couldn't break his quiz-show contract, so he was stuck playing Dr. Disaster.
WITH THE QUIZ SHOW CANCELLED, CARL IS FREE TO BE IN THE MOVIE AND BECOME A BIG STAR.
7
In the corner was the set for *Punk My Bike*. Once a week, Johnny Vile took the set apart to make room for the quiz show.
THAT BIKE HAS A DVD PLAYER! I WONDER IF IT COMES WITH A REMOTE.
PUNK MY BIKE
THAT'S A LOT OF TOOLS JUST TO FIX A BIKE.
IMPRESSIVE, ISN'T IT? I'VE BEEN HERE SINCE THIS MORNING PUTTING THIS SET TOGETHER FOR TONIGHT'S SHOW.
Johnny Vile didn't have much time to talk, but he did have a theory about the slime tank.
THAT FRIEND OF YOURS, BASHER, IS THE ONE WHO CUT THE BOLTS ON THE TANK. I SAW HIM MESSING WITH IT BEFORE THE SHOW.
THIS TV STUDIO HAS MORE GOSSIP THAN A SOAP OPERA!
THAT GOSSIP HAS HELPED ME SOLVE THE MYSTERY. I KNOW WHO SABOTAGED THE SLIME TANK.
Do you know who sent the slime sliding? Turn to page 79 for the solution.

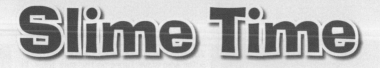

Slime Time

Uh-oh. When the slime tank burst, one of Zoe's crime scene files got slimed.

Use your detective skills and see if you can decipher this slimy page.

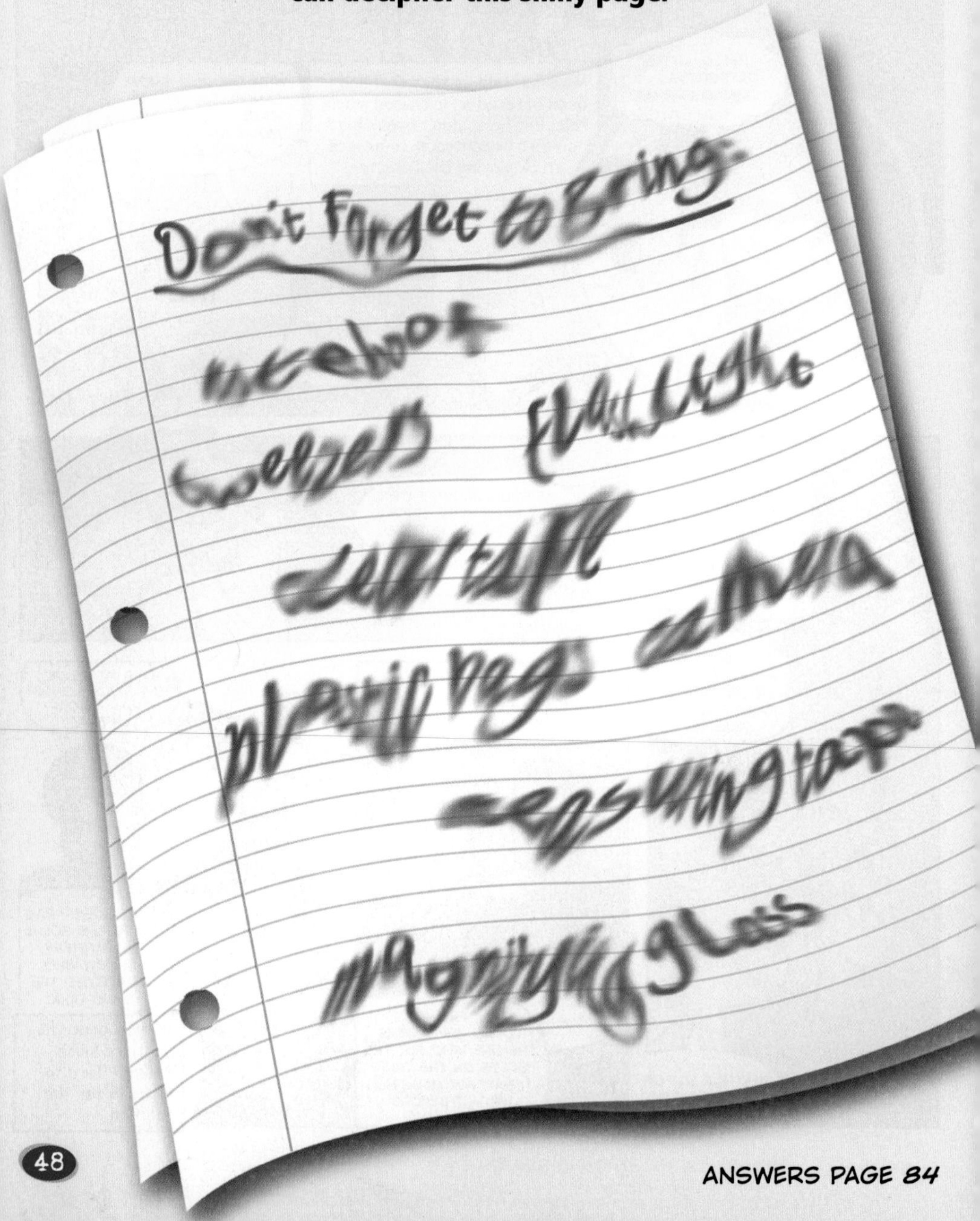

ANSWERS PAGE 84

LOST LOBSTER

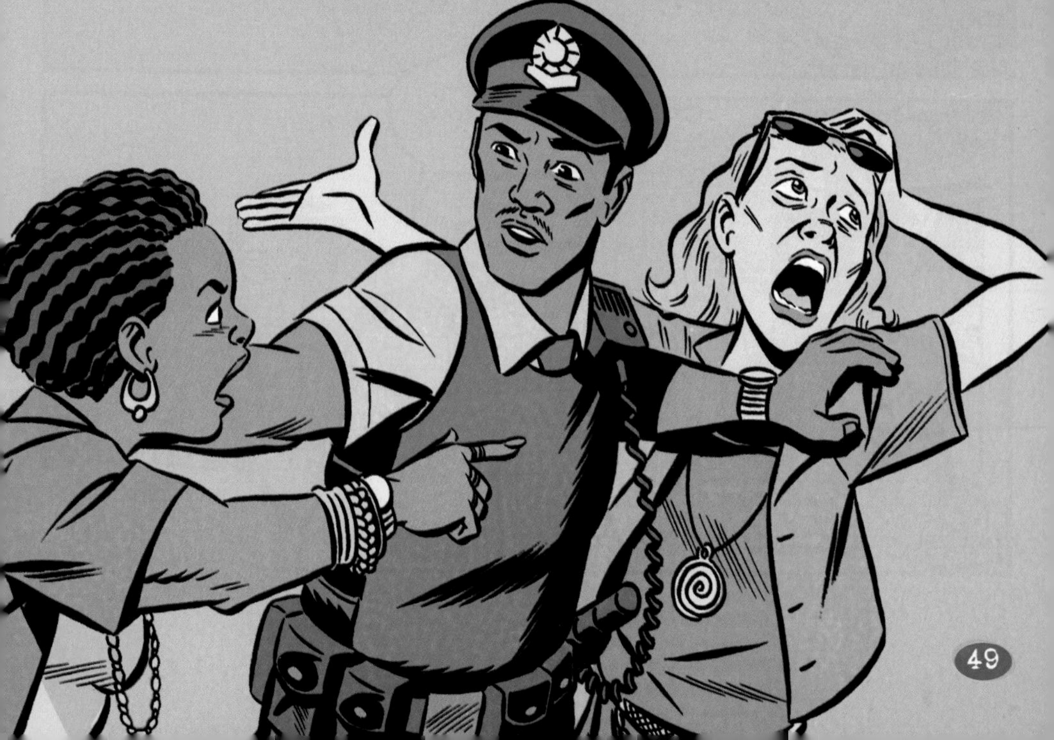

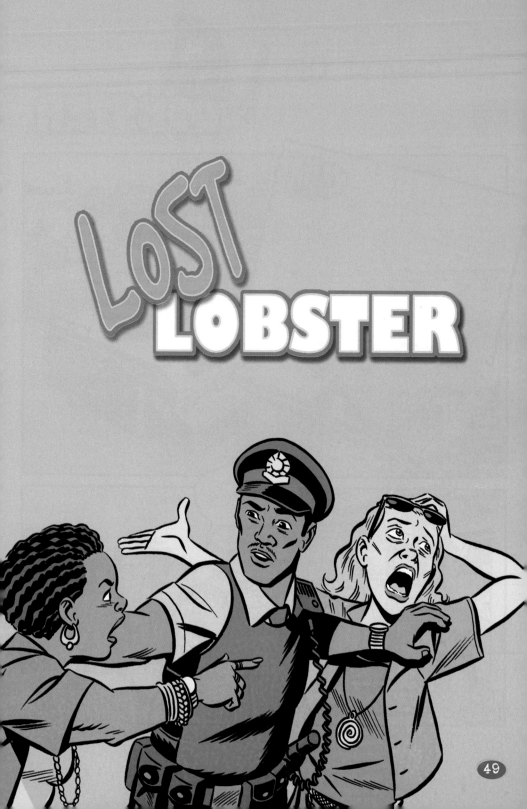

The Case of the LOST LOBSTER

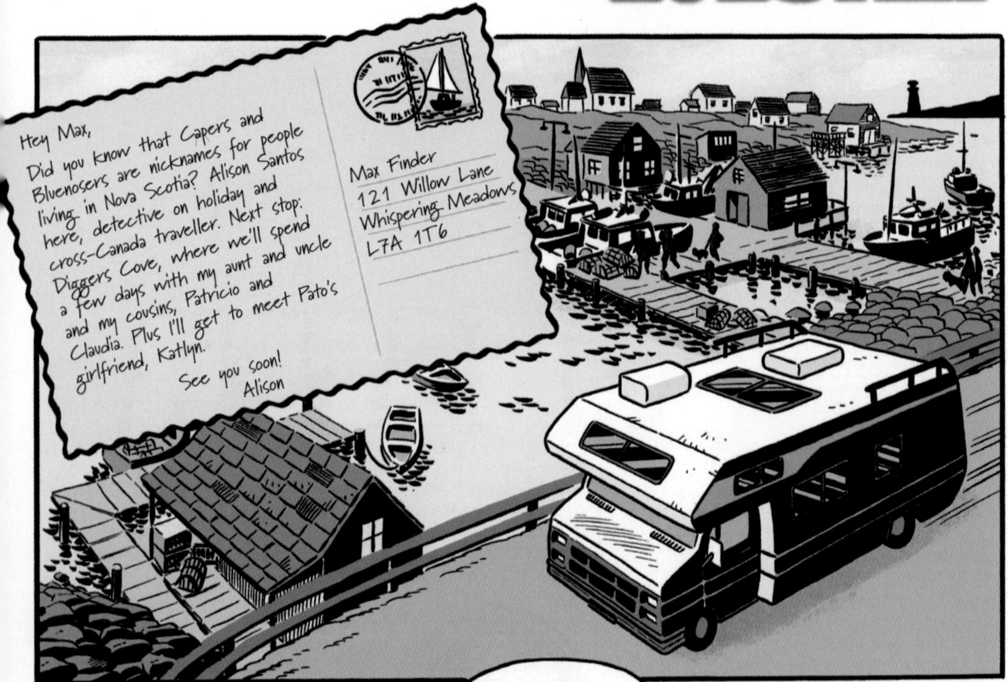

Hey Max,
Did you know that Capers and Bluenosers are nicknames for people living in Nova Scotia? Alison Santos here, detective on holiday and cross-Canada traveller. Next stop: Diggers Cove, where we'll spend a few days with my aunt and uncle and my cousins, Patricio and Claudia. Plus I'll get to meet Pato's girlfriend, Katlyn.
See you soon!
Alison
Max Finder
121 Willow Lane
Whispering Meadows
L7A 1T6

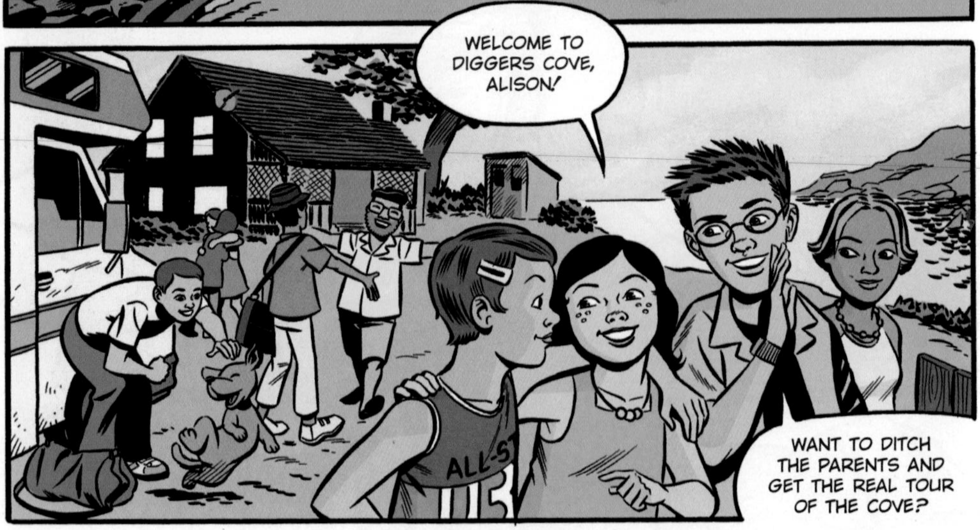

WELCOME TO DIGGERS COVE, ALISON!
WANT TO DITCH THE PARENTS AND GET THE REAL TOUR OF THE COVE?

LILLY'S LOBSTER HUT

HOME OF TWIGGY THE 2-TONE LOBSTER

LILLY'S LOBSTER HUT

TWIGGY

The harbour was beautiful, but I wasn't impressed with our first stop: the restaurant where Katlyn worked.

THAT LOBSTER LOOKS SO SAD, KATLYN.

TWIGGY

CRABLEGS SPECIAL TUESDAY

LILLY, THE OWNER, ONLY CARES ABOUT ATTRACTING TOURISTS. SHE'S AFRAID TWIGGY WILL CLIMB OUT OF THE TANK AND BITE HER.

KUNG FU DOUBLE FEATURE WED-FRI

SEE YOU TWO WHEN YOU'RE FINISHED WORK. WE'VE GOT TO GET HOME FOR DINNER.

The next morning, Claudia and I headed back downtown.

ALISON! SOMEONE STOLE TWIGGY THE LOBSTER!

LILLY'S LOBSTER HUT

HUT HOME OF GGY THE LOBSTER

TWIGGY

KUNG-FU DOUBLE FEATURE WED-FRI

51

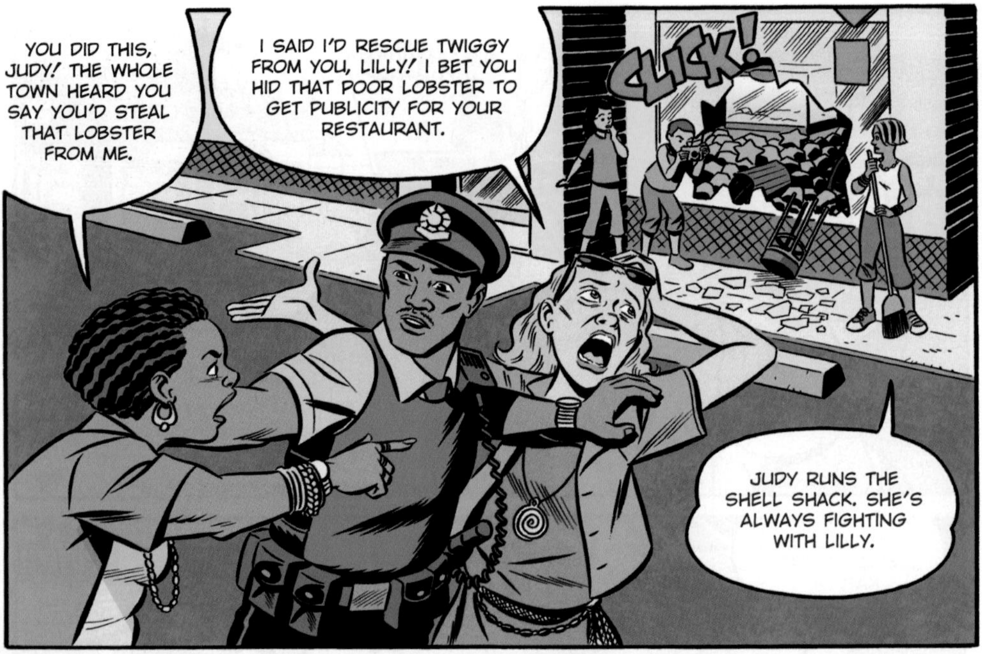
YOU DID THIS, JUDY! THE WHOLE TOWN HEARD YOU SAY YOU'D STEAL THAT LOBSTER FROM ME.
I SAID I'D RESCUE TWIGGY FROM YOU, LILLY! I BET YOU HID THAT POOR LOBSTER TO GET PUBLICITY FOR YOUR RESTAURANT.
CLICK!
JUDY RUNS THE SHELL SHACK. SHE'S ALWAYS FIGHTING WITH LILLY.

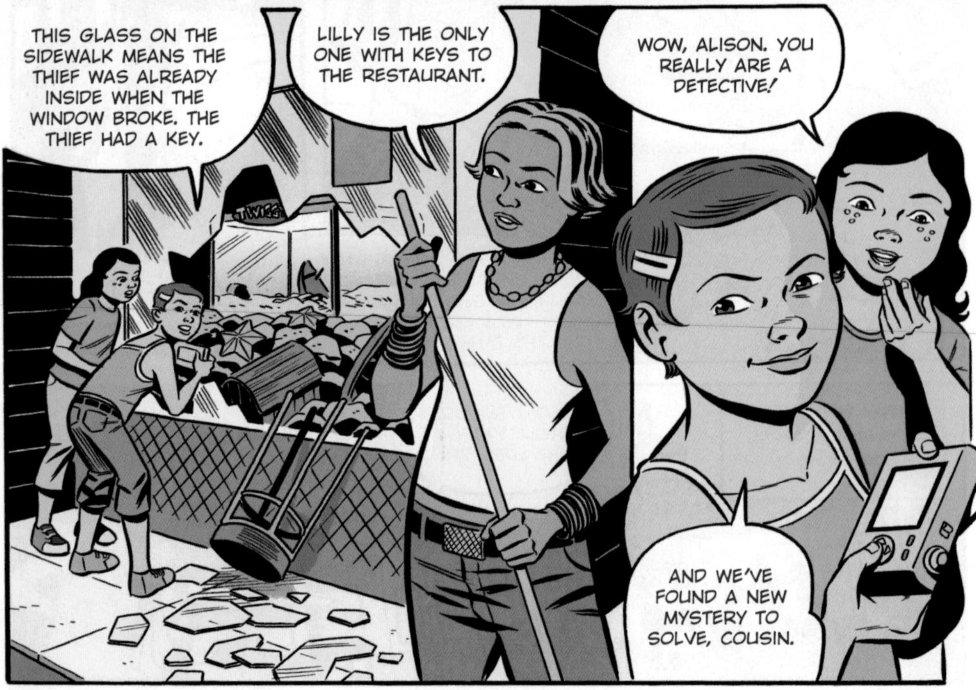
THIS GLASS ON THE SIDEWALK MEANS THE THIEF WAS ALREADY INSIDE WHEN THE WINDOW BROKE. THE THIEF HAD A KEY.
LILLY IS THE ONLY ONE WITH KEYS TO THE RESTAURANT.
WOW, ALISON. YOU REALLY ARE A DETECTIVE!
AND WE'VE FOUND A NEW MYSTERY TO SOLVE, COUSIN.

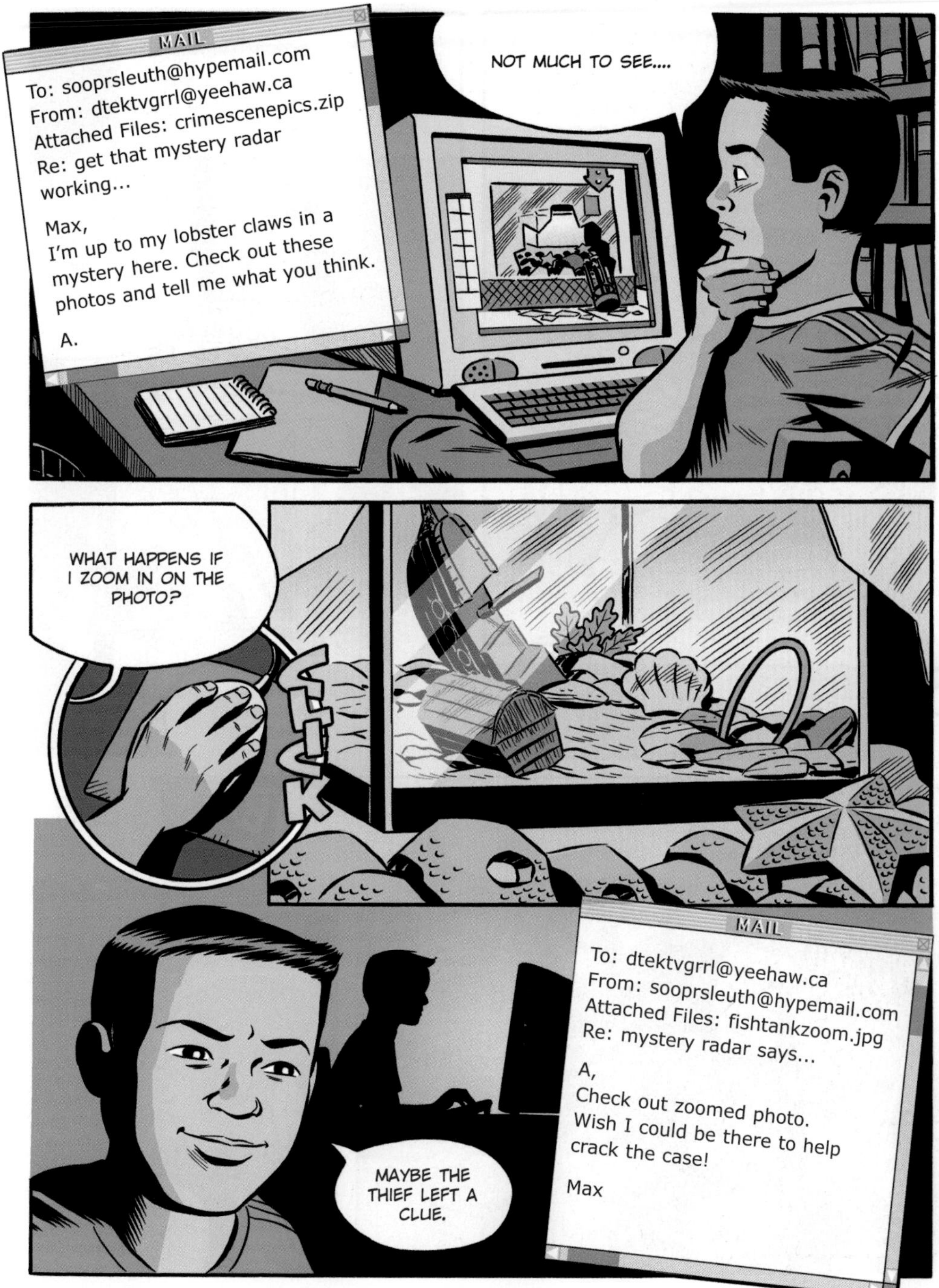
MAIL
To: sooprsleuth@hypemail.com
From: dtektvgrrl@yeehaw.ca
Attached Files: crimescenepics.zip
Re: get that mystery radar working...
Max,
I'm up to my lobster claws in a mystery here. Check out these photos and tell me what you think.
A.
NOT MUCH TO SEE....
WHAT HAPPENS IF I ZOOM IN ON THE PHOTO?
CLICK
MAIL
To: dtektvgrrl@yeehaw.ca
From: sooprsleuth@hypemail.com
Attached Files: fishtankzoom.jpg
Re: mystery radar says...
A,
Check out zoomed photo.
Wish I could be there to help crack the case!
Max
MAYBE THE THIEF LEFT A CLUE.

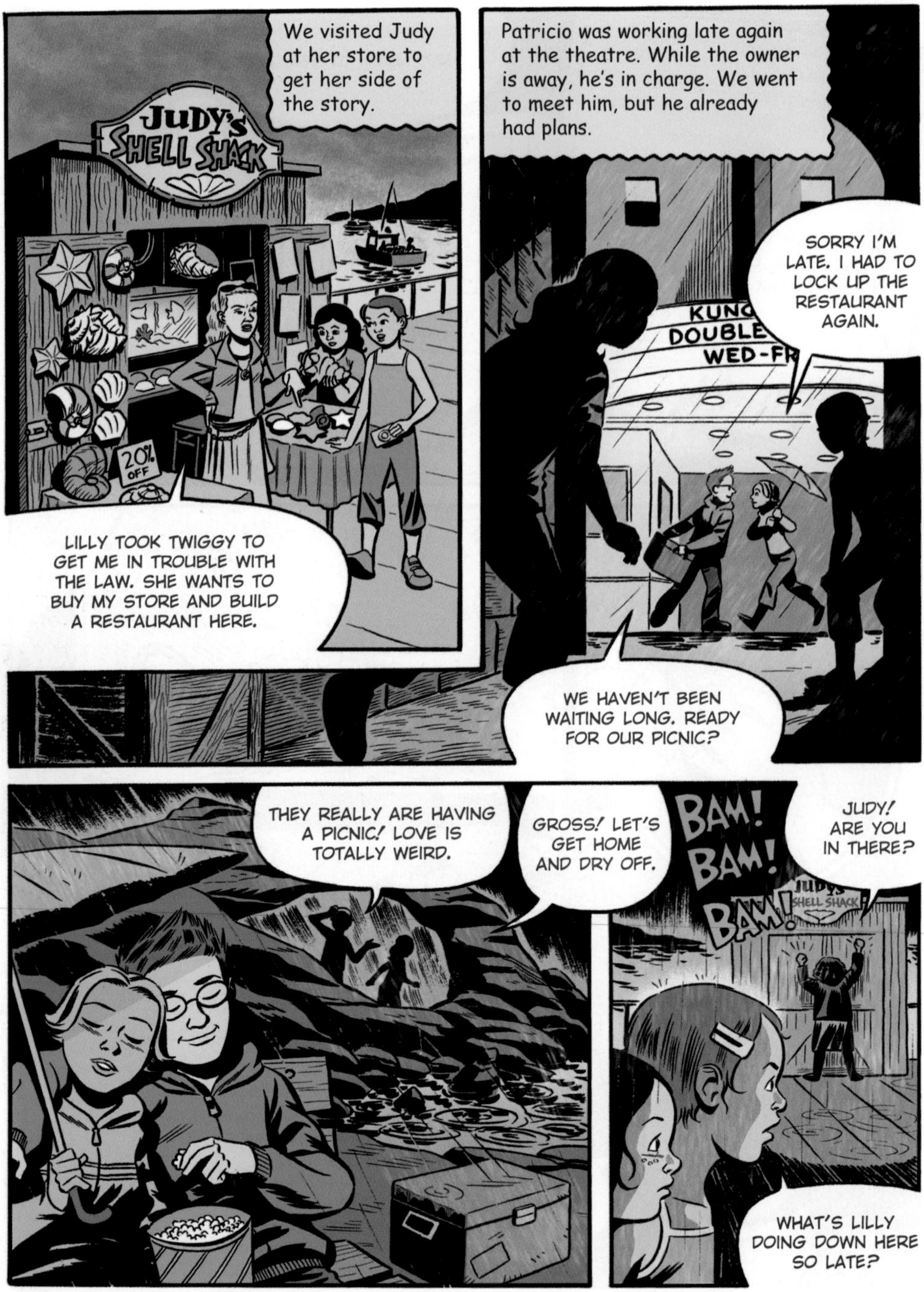

We visited Judy at her store to get her side of the story.
JUDY'S SHELL SHACK
20% OFF
LILLY TOOK TWIGGY TO GET ME IN TROUBLE WITH THE LAW. SHE WANTS TO BUY MY STORE AND BUILD A RESTAURANT HERE.
Patricio was working late again at the theatre. While the owner is away, he's in charge. We went to meet him, but he already had plans.
SORRY I'M LATE. I HAD TO LOCK UP THE RESTAURANT AGAIN.
WE HAVEN'T BEEN WAITING LONG. READY FOR OUR PICNIC?
THEY REALLY ARE HAVING A PICNIC! LOVE IS TOTALLY WEIRD.
GROSS! LET'S GET HOME AND DRY OFF.
BAM! BAM! BAM!
JUDY'S SHELL SHACK
JUDY! ARE YOU IN THERE?
WHAT'S LILLY DOING DOWN HERE SO LATE?

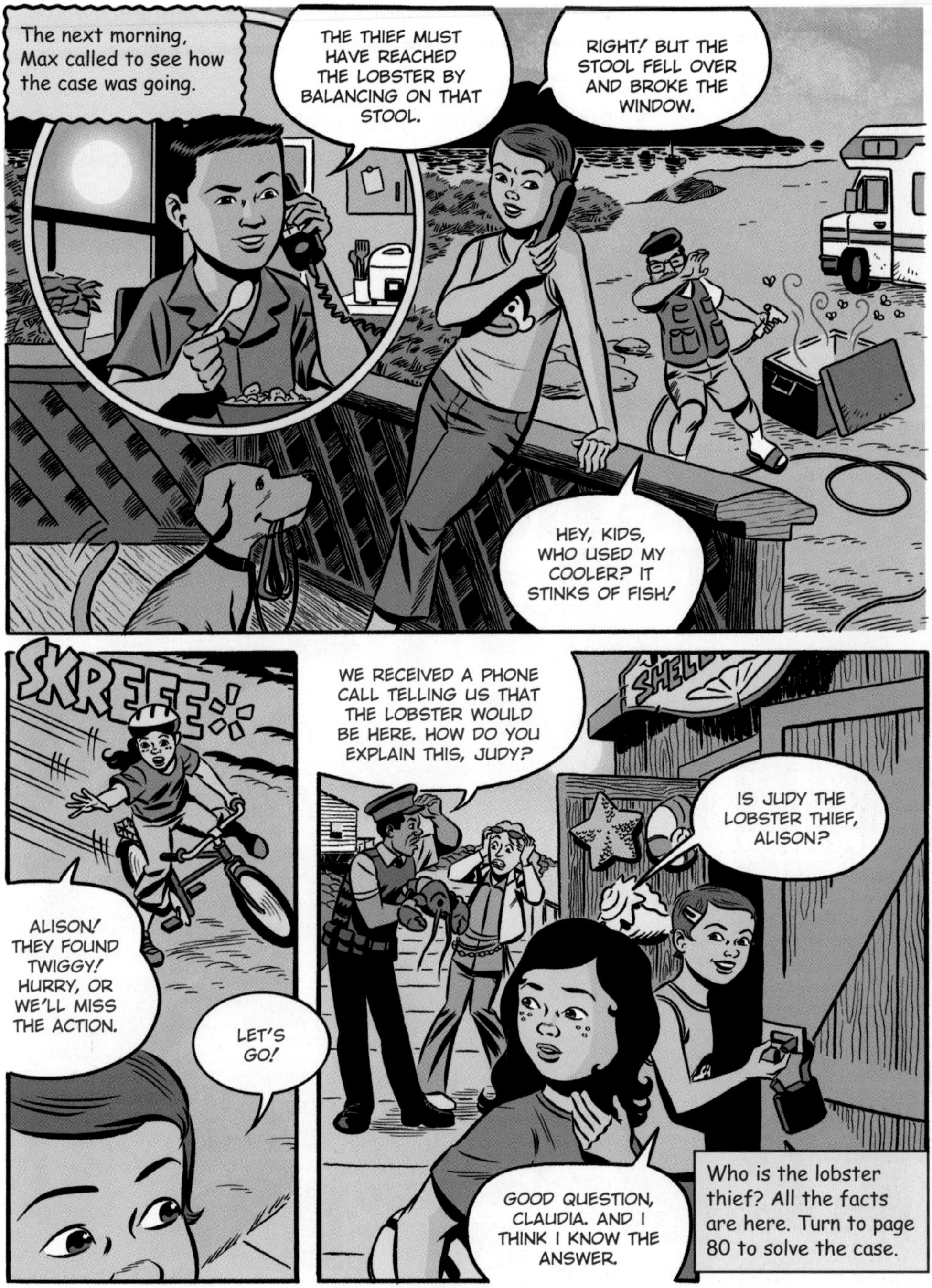
The next morning, Max called to see how the case was going.
THE THIEF MUST HAVE REACHED THE LOBSTER BY BALANCING ON THAT STOOL.
RIGHT! BUT THE STOOL FELL OVER AND BROKE THE WINDOW.
HEY, KIDS, WHO USED MY COOLER? IT STINKS OF FISH!
SKREEE!
ALISON! THEY FOUND TWIGGY! HURRY, OR WE'LL MISS THE ACTION.
LET'S GO!
WE RECEIVED A PHONE CALL TELLING US THAT THE LOBSTER WOULD BE HERE. HOW DO YOU EXPLAIN THIS, JUDY?
IS JUDY THE LOBSTER THIEF, ALISON?
GOOD QUESTION, CLAUDIA. AND I THINK I KNOW THE ANSWER.
Who is the lobster thief? All the facts are here. Turn to page 80 to solve the case.

Stick with It

Max has added the stamp from Alison's postcard to his stamp collection. **Have a look at all of his stamps and see if you can find:**

1. the three identical stamps
2. the stamp that appears upside down and backwards
3. the stamp from Zimbabwe
4. the stamp with a lighthouse on it
5. the stamp worth fifteen cents

How many Canadian stamps are in Max's collection?

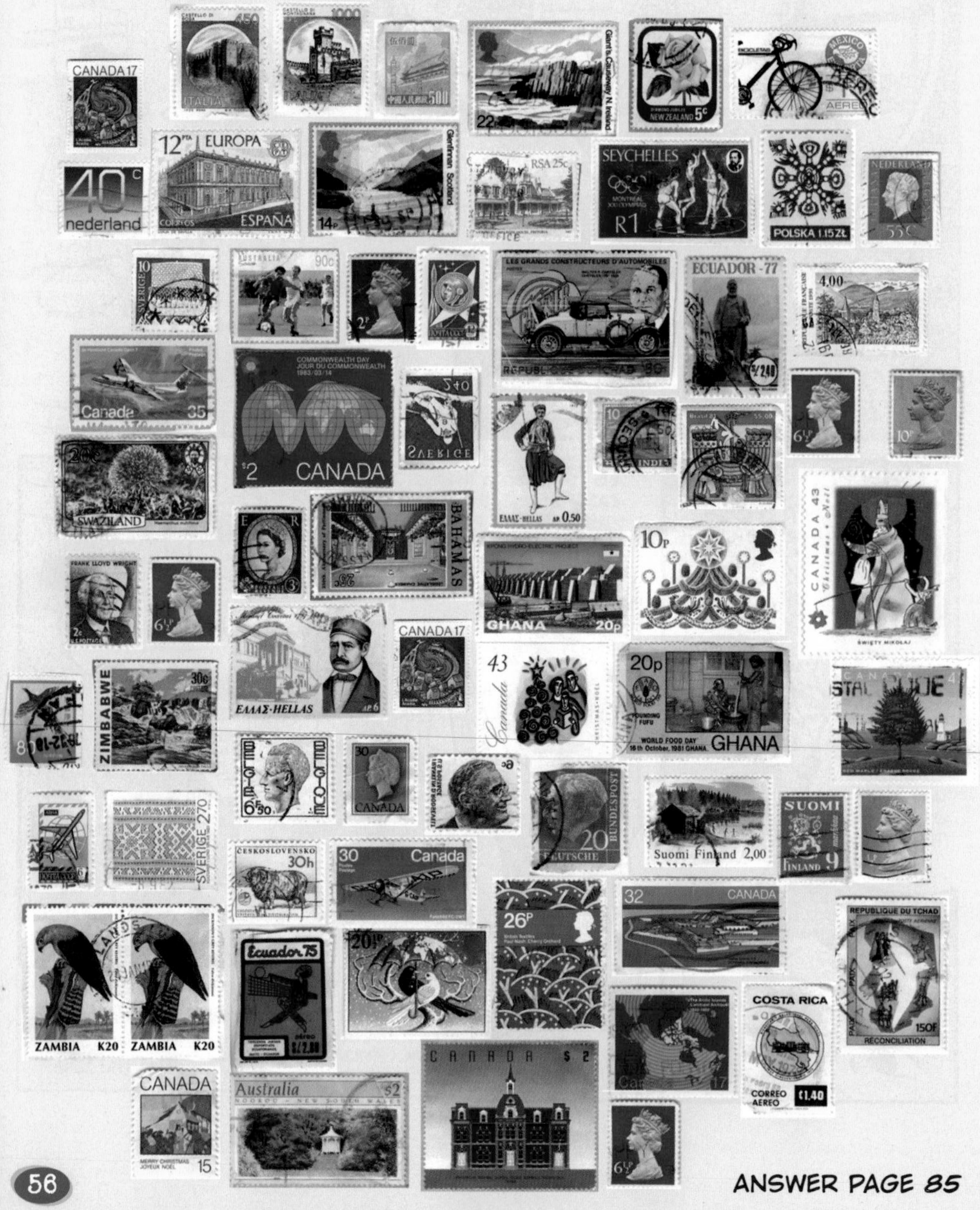
CANADA 17
ITALIA
12 EUROPA
ESPAÑA
40 c nederland
NEW ZEALAND 5c
SEYCHELLES R1
POLSKA 1.15 Zł
RSA 25c
ECUADOR-77
Canada 35
$2 CANADA
COMMONWEALTH DAY
SVERIGE
SWAZILAND
BAHAMAS
ΕΛΛΑΣ-HELLAS 0.50
GHANA 20p
10p
CANADA 43
CANADA 17
43 Canada
20p
WORLD FOOD DAY
GHANA
ZIMBABWE
ΕΛΛΑΣ·HELLAS
CANADA
DEUTSCHE BUNDESPOST 20
Suomi Finland 2,00
SUOMI FINLAND 9
SVERIGE 270
ČESKOSLOVENSKO 30h
30 Canada
ZAMBIA K20
ZAMBIA K20
Ecuador 75
26p
32 CANADA
REPUBLIQUE DU TCHAD
RECONCILIATION
COSTA RICA
CORREO AEREO
CANADA
MERRY CHRISTMAS JOYEUX NOEL 15
Australia $2
CANADA $2
2p
6½p
10p

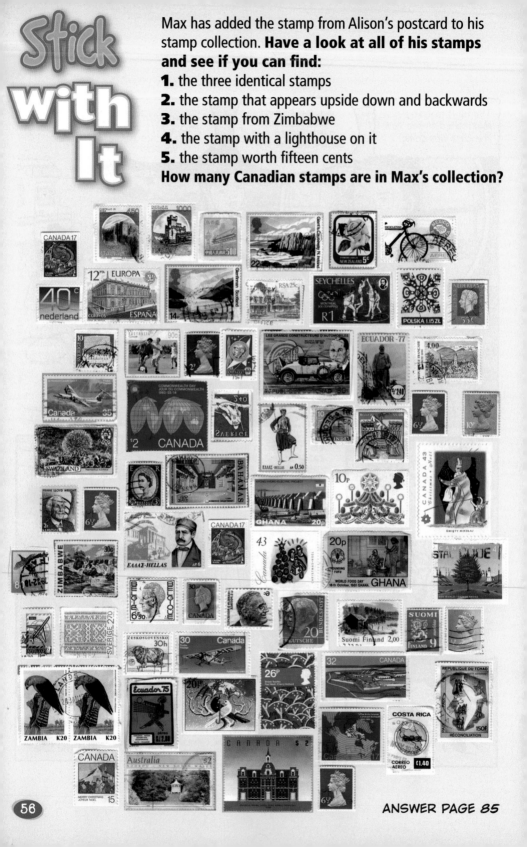

ANSWER PAGE 85

Movie Set Mischief

The Case of the Movie Set Mischief

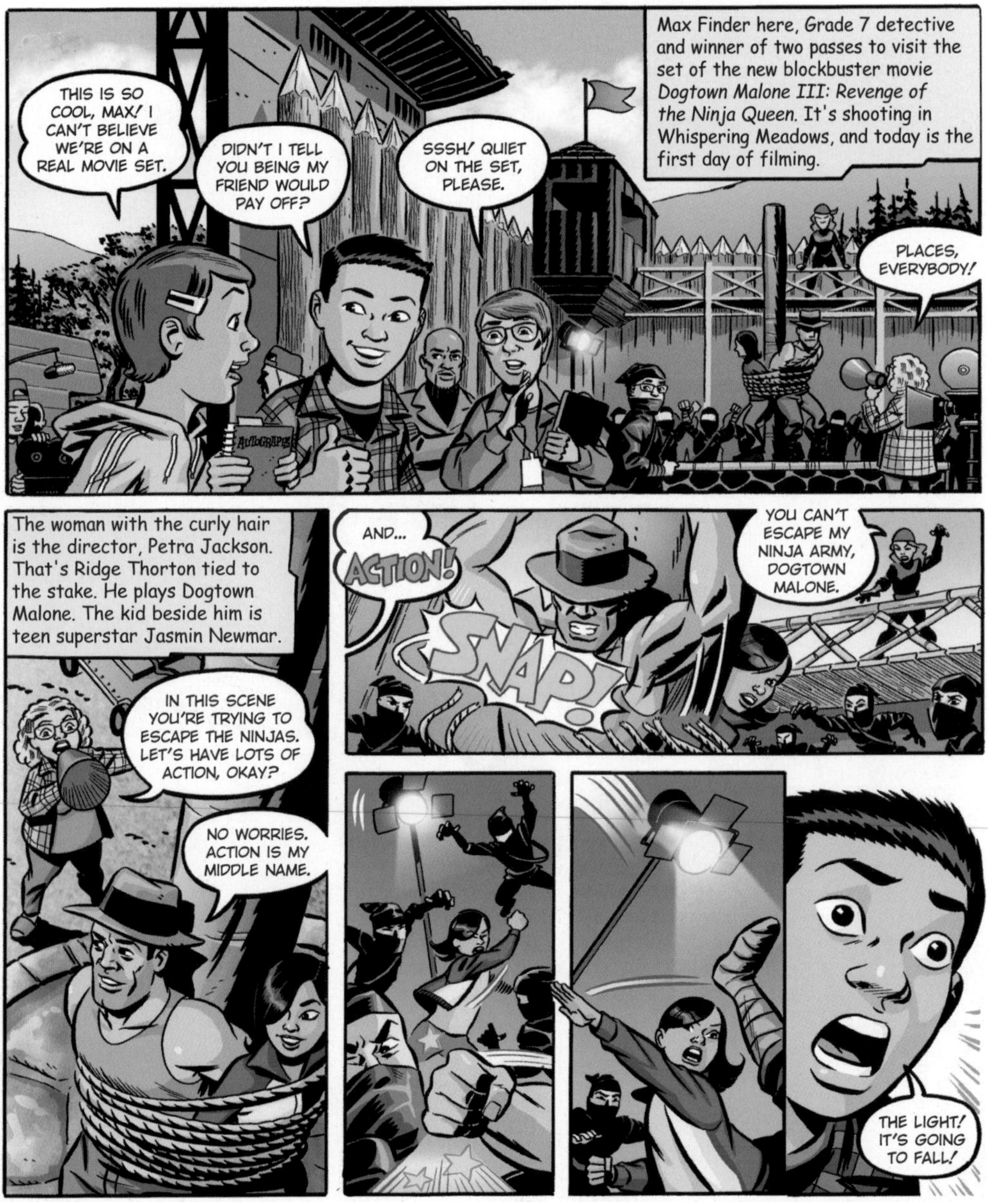
Max Finder here, Grade 7 detective and winner of two passes to visit the set of the new blockbuster movie *Dogtown Malone III: Revenge of the Ninja Queen*. It's shooting in Whispering Meadows, and today is the first day of filming.
THIS IS SO COOL, MAX! I CAN'T BELIEVE WE'RE ON A REAL MOVIE SET.
DIDN'T I TELL YOU BEING MY FRIEND WOULD PAY OFF?
SSSH! QUIET ON THE SET, PLEASE.
PLACES, EVERYBODY!
AUTOGRAPHS
The woman with the curly hair is the director, Petra Jackson. That's Ridge Thorton tied to the stake. He plays Dogtown Malone. The kid beside him is teen superstar Jasmin Newmar.
IN THIS SCENE YOU'RE TRYING TO ESCAPE THE NINJAS. LET'S HAVE LOTS OF ACTION, OKAY?
NO WORRIES. ACTION IS MY MIDDLE NAME.
AND... ACTION!
SNAP!
YOU CAN'T ESCAPE MY NINJA ARMY, DOGTOWN MALONE.
THE LIGHT! IT'S GOING TO FALL!

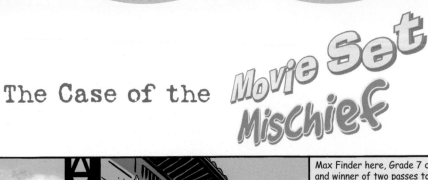

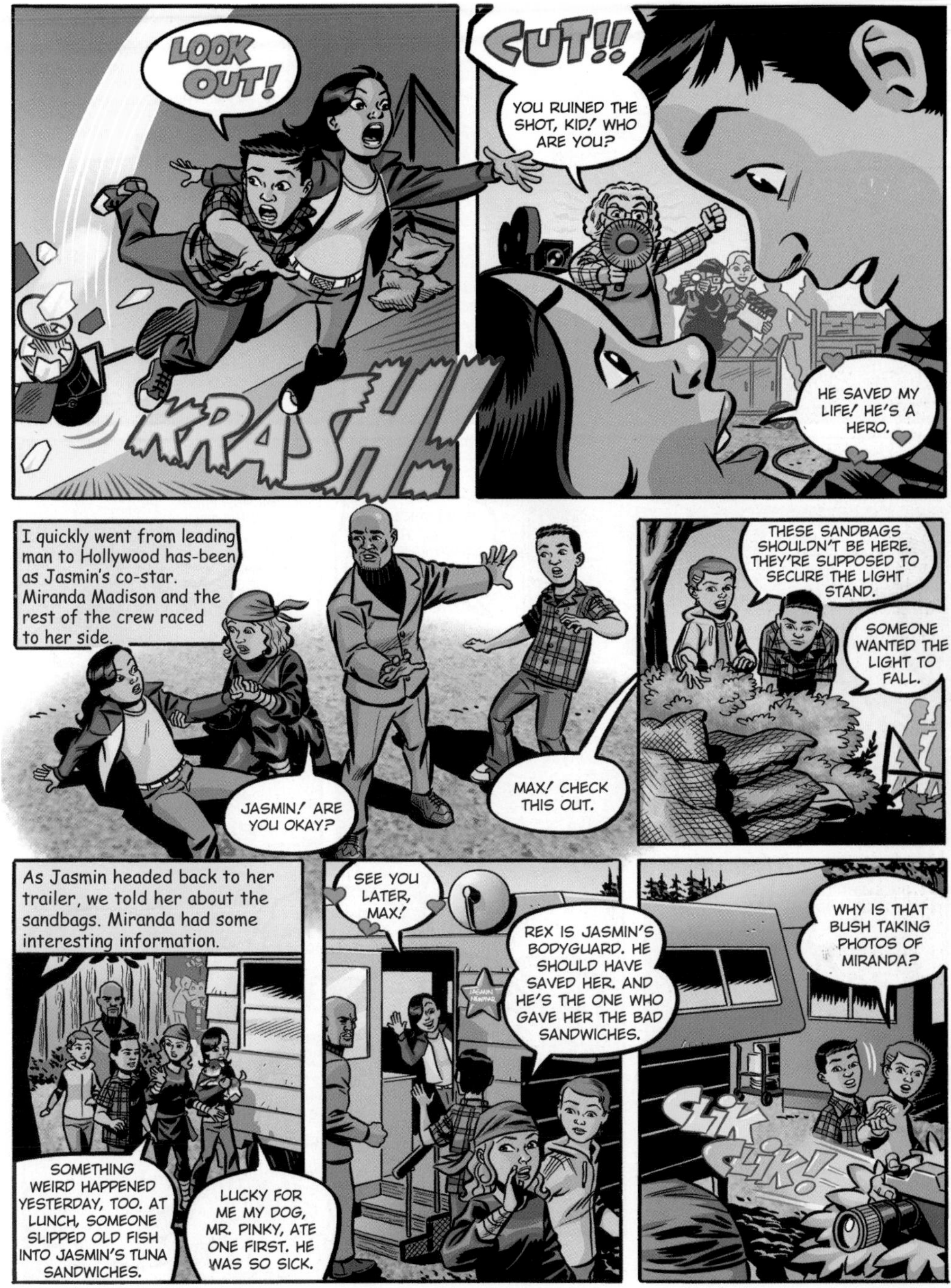
LOOK OUT!
KRASH!
CUT!!
YOU RUINED THE SHOT, KID! WHO ARE YOU?
HE SAVED MY LIFE! HE'S A HERO.
I quickly went from leading man to Hollywood has-been as Jasmin's co-star. Miranda Madison and the rest of the crew raced to her side.
JASMIN! ARE YOU OKAY?
MAX! CHECK THIS OUT.
THESE SANDBAGS SHOULDN'T BE HERE. THEY'RE SUPPOSED TO SECURE THE LIGHT STAND.
SOMEONE WANTED THE LIGHT TO FALL.
As Jasmin headed back to her trailer, we told her about the sandbags. Miranda had some interesting information.
SOMETHING WEIRD HAPPENED YESTERDAY, TOO. AT LUNCH, SOMEONE SLIPPED OLD FISH INTO JASMIN'S TUNA SANDWICHES.
LUCKY FOR ME MY DOG, MR. PINKY, ATE ONE FIRST. HE WAS SO SICK.
SEE YOU LATER, MAX!
REX IS JASMIN'S BODYGUARD. HE SHOULD HAVE SAVED HER. AND HE'S THE ONE WHO GAVE HER THE BAD SANDWICHES.
WHY IS THAT BUSH TAKING PHOTOS OF MIRANDA?
CLIK CLIK!

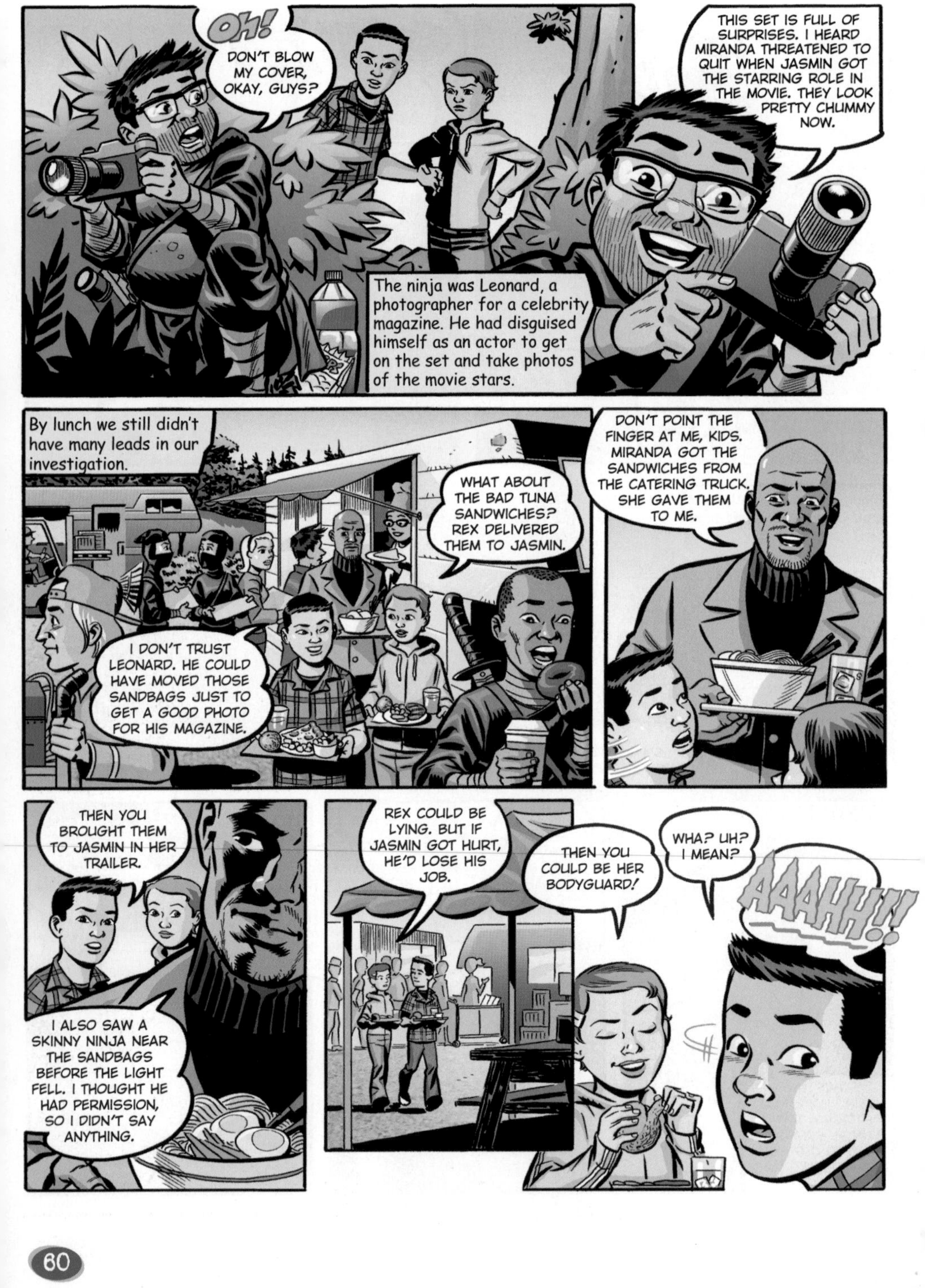
OH!
DON'T BLOW MY COVER, OKAY, GUYS?
THIS SET IS FULL OF SURPRISES. I HEARD MIRANDA THREATENED TO QUIT WHEN JASMIN GOT THE STARRING ROLE IN THE MOVIE. THEY LOOK PRETTY CHUMMY NOW.
The ninja was Leonard, a photographer for a celebrity magazine. He had disguised himself as an actor to get on the set and take photos of the movie stars.
By lunch we still didn't have many leads in our investigation.
I DON'T TRUST LEONARD. HE COULD HAVE MOVED THOSE SANDBAGS JUST TO GET A GOOD PHOTO FOR HIS MAGAZINE.
WHAT ABOUT THE BAD TUNA SANDWICHES? REX DELIVERED THEM TO JASMIN.
DON'T POINT THE FINGER AT ME, KIDS. MIRANDA GOT THE SANDWICHES FROM THE CATERING TRUCK. SHE GAVE THEM TO ME.
THEN YOU BROUGHT THEM TO JASMIN IN HER TRAILER.
I ALSO SAW A SKINNY NINJA NEAR THE SANDBAGS BEFORE THE LIGHT FELL. I THOUGHT HE HAD PERMISSION, SO I DIDN'T SAY ANYTHING.
REX COULD BE LYING. BUT IF JASMIN GOT HURT, HE'D LOSE HIS JOB.
THEN YOU COULD BE HER BODYGUARD!
WHA? UH? I MEAN?
AAAHH!!

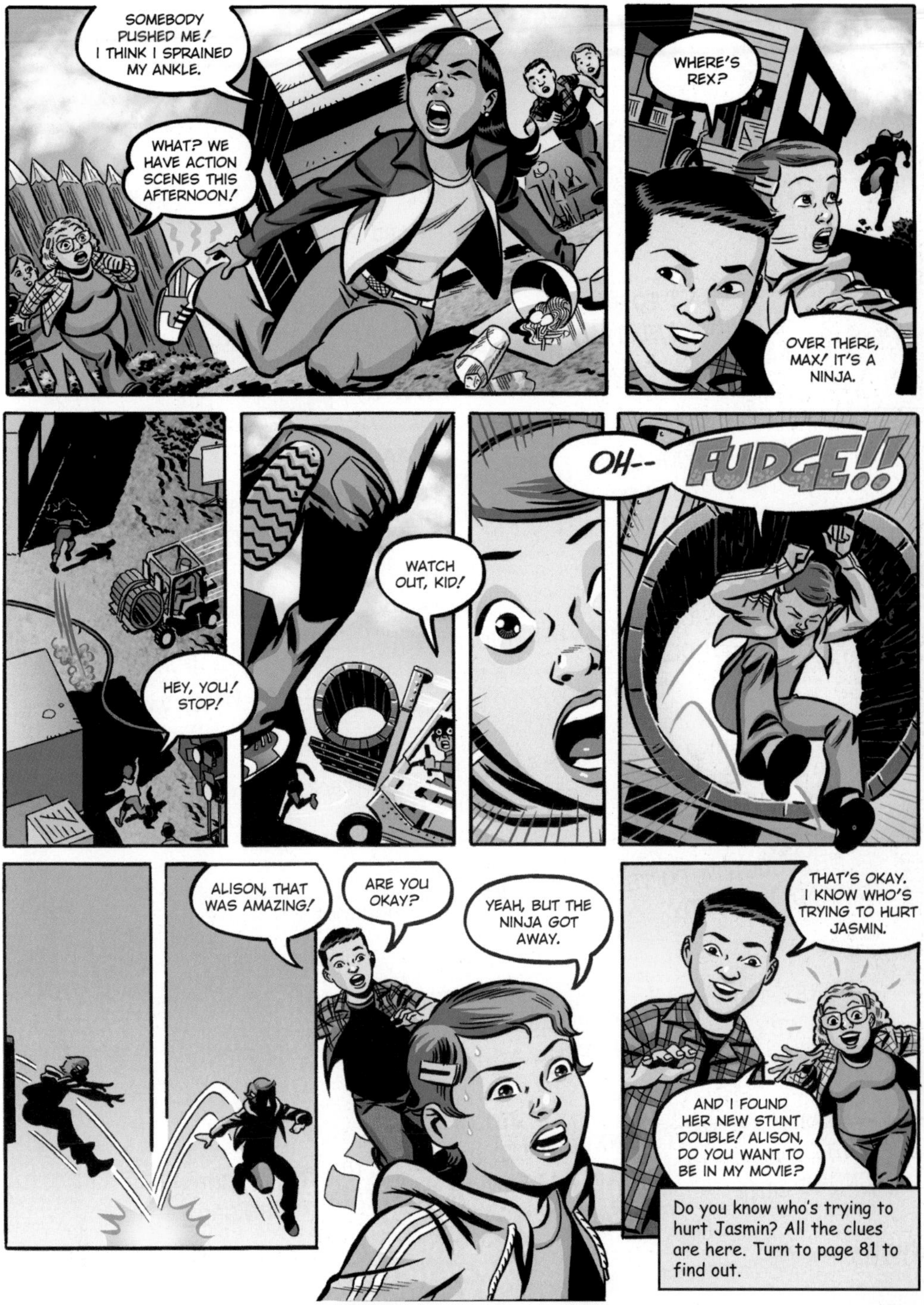
SOMEBODY PUSHED ME! I THINK I SPRAINED MY ANKLE.
WHAT? WE HAVE ACTION SCENES THIS AFTERNOON!
WHERE'S REX?
OVER THERE, MAX! IT'S A NINJA.
HEY, YOU! STOP!
WATCH OUT, KID!
OH-- FUDGE!!
ALISON, THAT WAS AMAZING!
ARE YOU OKAY?
YEAH, BUT THE NINJA GOT AWAY.
THAT'S OKAY. I KNOW WHO'S TRYING TO HURT JASMIN.
AND I FOUND HER NEW STUNT DOUBLE! ALISON, DO YOU WANT TO BE IN MY MOVIE?
Do you know who's trying to hurt Jasmin? All the clues are here. Turn to page 81 to find out.

It's your turn to make it in the movie business. **Complete the blanks in this Dogtown Malone movie script. Then read it aloud. Have a friend do the same.**

Scene 6:

A ninja army has captured Dogtown Malone and Julia. They want the pair to reveal the secret of the lost [a vegetable]. The army has locked them in a [name of an appliance] and left.

MALONE

WE'VE GOT TO ESCAPE BEFORE THAT ARMY OF [clothing item] RETURNS AND TRIES TO MAKE US TALK. LET'S TRY TO BREAK THESE [school supply] AND MAKE OUR WAY TO [planet].

JULIA

WE'LL NEVER MAKE IT. WE DON'T HAVE A [wild animal] OR EVEN A [kid's toy]. I TOLD YOU WE SHOULD HAVE BROUGHT [famous athlete] WITH US.

MALONE

DON'T PANIC. YOU'RE STARTING TO SOUND LIKE A [type of fish] IN THE MIDDLE OF [name of a month]. LET'S THINK: WHAT WOULD [name of superhero] DO?

Malone hands Julia a [type of bug] from his backpack. But she reaches in her pocket for a [piece of furniture] instead.

JULIA

THIS OUGHTA DO THE TRICK. I KNEW A [name of a flower] WOULD COME IN HANDY.

MALONE

HURRY, THEY'RE COMING. THROW ME THAT [something smelly] AND WE'LL RACE TO [favourite amusment park].

JULIA

GREAT IDEA! THEY'LL NEVER FIND US THERE. UNLESS, OF COURSE, THE [favourite sports team] ARE IN ON THIS. THEN WE'RE SURE TO END UP LIKE [type of junk food].

Hijacked Hat

The Case of the Hijacked Hat

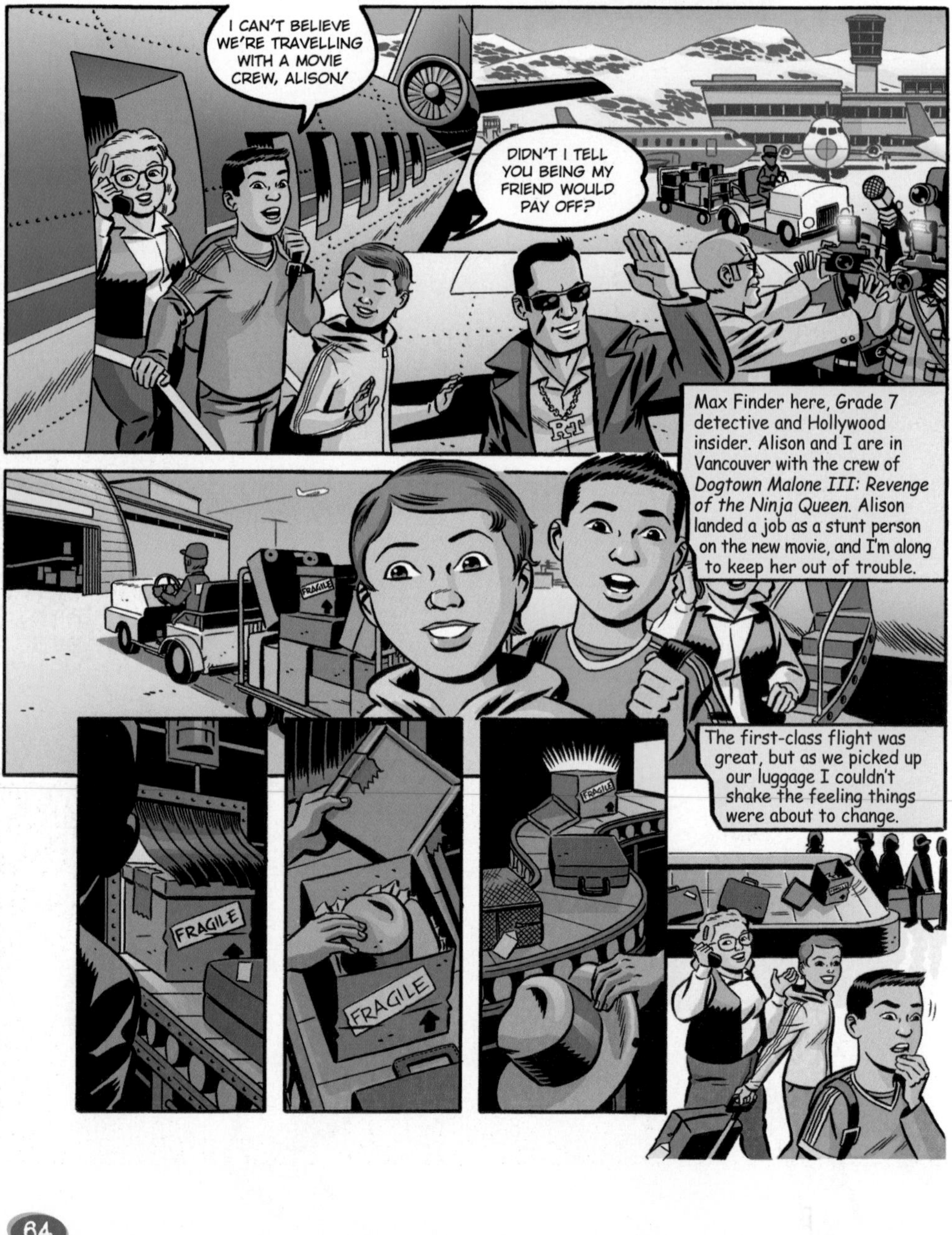
I CAN'T BELIEVE WE'RE TRAVELLING WITH A MOVIE CREW, ALISON!
DIDN'T I TELL YOU BEING MY FRIEND WOULD PAY OFF?
Max Finder here, Grade 7 detective and Hollywood insider. Alison and I are in Vancouver with the crew of *Dogtown Malone III: Revenge of the Ninja Queen.* Alison landed a job as a stunt person on the new movie, and I'm along to keep her out of trouble.
FRAGILE
The first-class flight was great, but as we picked up our luggage I couldn't shake the feeling things were about to change.
FRAGILE
FRAGILE
FRAGILE

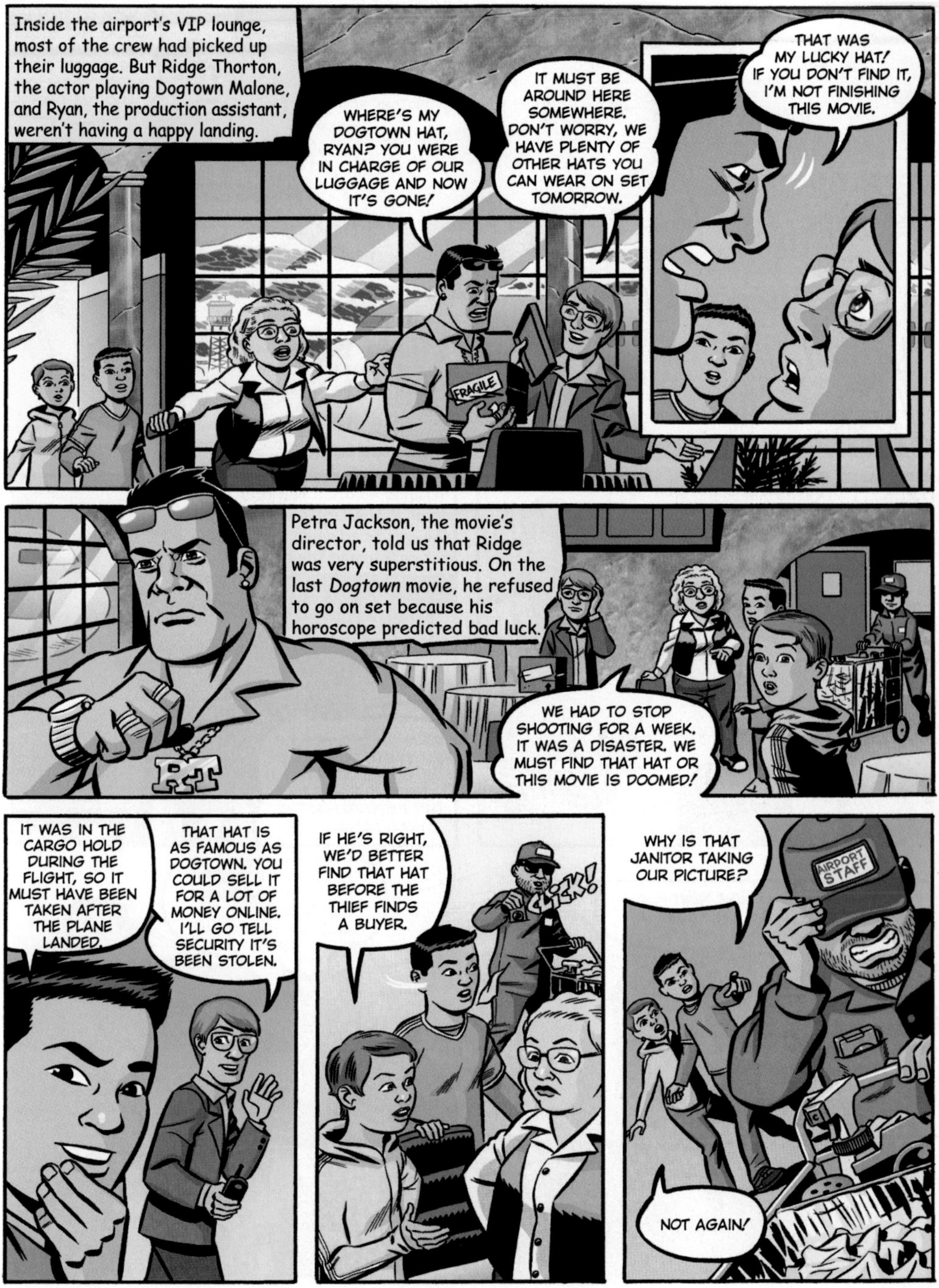
Inside the airport's VIP lounge, most of the crew had picked up their luggage. But Ridge Thorton, the actor playing Dogtown Malone, and Ryan, the production assistant, weren't having a happy landing.
WHERE'S MY DOGTOWN HAT, RYAN? YOU WERE IN CHARGE OF OUR LUGGAGE AND NOW IT'S GONE!
IT MUST BE AROUND HERE SOMEWHERE. DON'T WORRY, WE HAVE PLENTY OF OTHER HATS YOU CAN WEAR ON SET TOMORROW.
THAT WAS MY LUCKY HAT! IF YOU DON'T FIND IT, I'M NOT FINISHING THIS MOVIE.
FRAGILE
Petra Jackson, the movie's director, told us that Ridge was very superstitious. On the last *Dogtown* movie, he refused to go on set because his horoscope predicted bad luck.
WE HAD TO STOP SHOOTING FOR A WEEK. IT WAS A DISASTER. WE MUST FIND THAT HAT OR THIS MOVIE IS DOOMED!
RT
IT WAS IN THE CARGO HOLD DURING THE FLIGHT, SO IT MUST HAVE BEEN TAKEN AFTER THE PLANE LANDED.
THAT HAT IS AS FAMOUS AS DOGTOWN. YOU COULD SELL IT FOR A LOT OF MONEY ONLINE. I'LL GO TELL SECURITY IT'S BEEN STOLEN.
IF HE'S RIGHT, WE'D BETTER FIND THAT HAT BEFORE THE THIEF FINDS A BUYER.
CLICK!
WHY IS THAT JANITOR TAKING OUR PICTURE?
AIRPORT STAFF
NOT AGAIN!

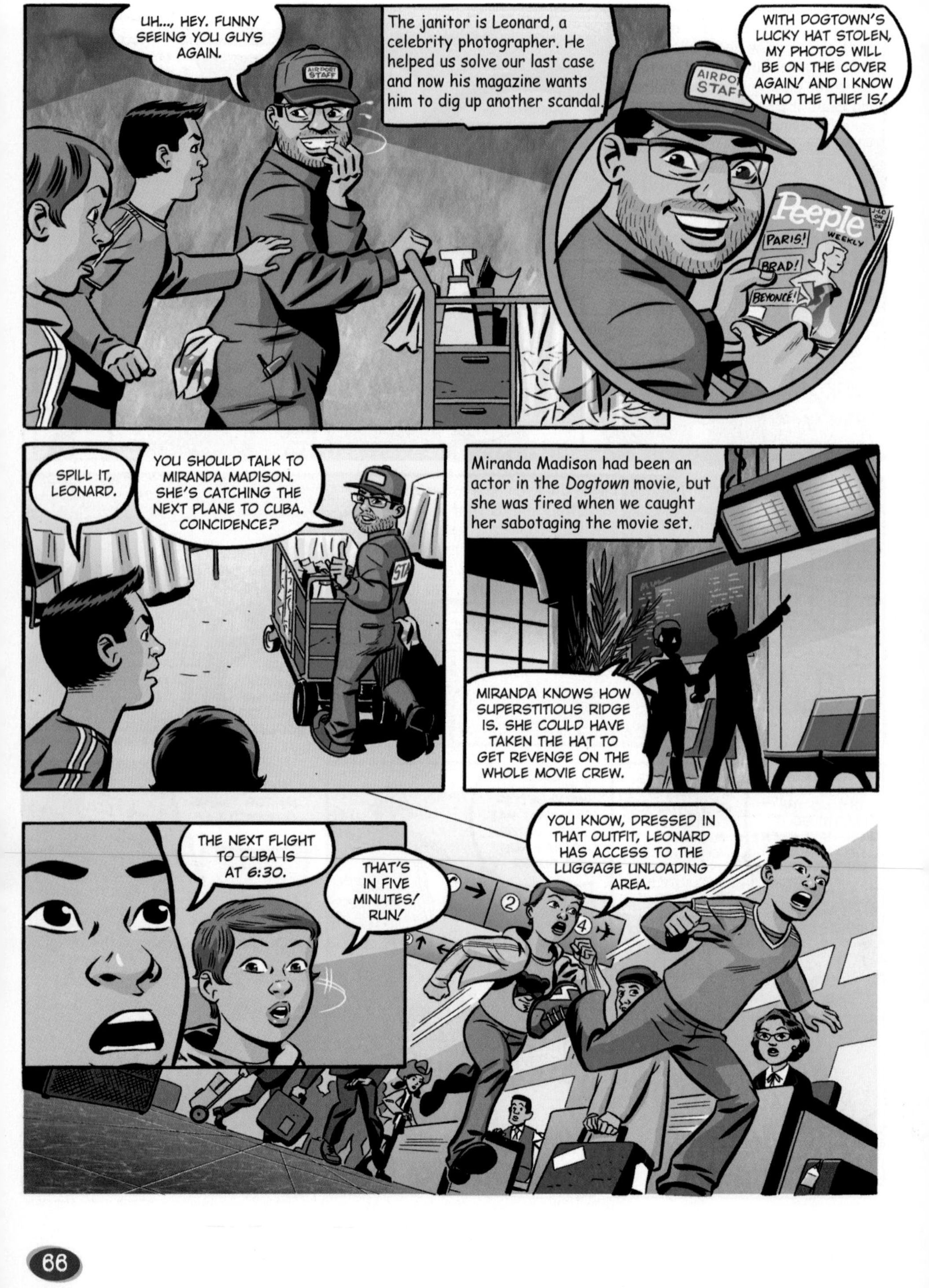
UH..., HEY. FUNNY SEEING YOU GUYS AGAIN.
AIRPORT STAFF
The janitor is Leonard, a celebrity photographer. He helped us solve our last case and now his magazine wants him to dig up another scandal.
WITH DOGTOWN'S LUCKY HAT STOLEN, MY PHOTOS WILL BE ON THE COVER AGAIN! AND I KNOW WHO THE THIEF IS!
AIRPORT STAFF
Peeple
WEEKLY
PARIS!
BRAD!
BEYONCÉ!
SPILL IT, LEONARD.
YOU SHOULD TALK TO MIRANDA MADISON. SHE'S CATCHING THE NEXT PLANE TO CUBA. COINCIDENCE?
Miranda Madison had been an actor in the *Dogtown* movie, but she was fired when we caught her sabotaging the movie set.
MIRANDA KNOWS HOW SUPERSTITIOUS RIDGE IS. SHE COULD HAVE TAKEN THE HAT TO GET REVENGE ON THE WHOLE MOVIE CREW.
THE NEXT FLIGHT TO CUBA IS AT 6:30.
THAT'S IN FIVE MINUTES! RUN!
YOU KNOW, DRESSED IN THAT OUTFIT, LEONARD HAS ACCESS TO THE LUGGAGE UNLOADING AREA.

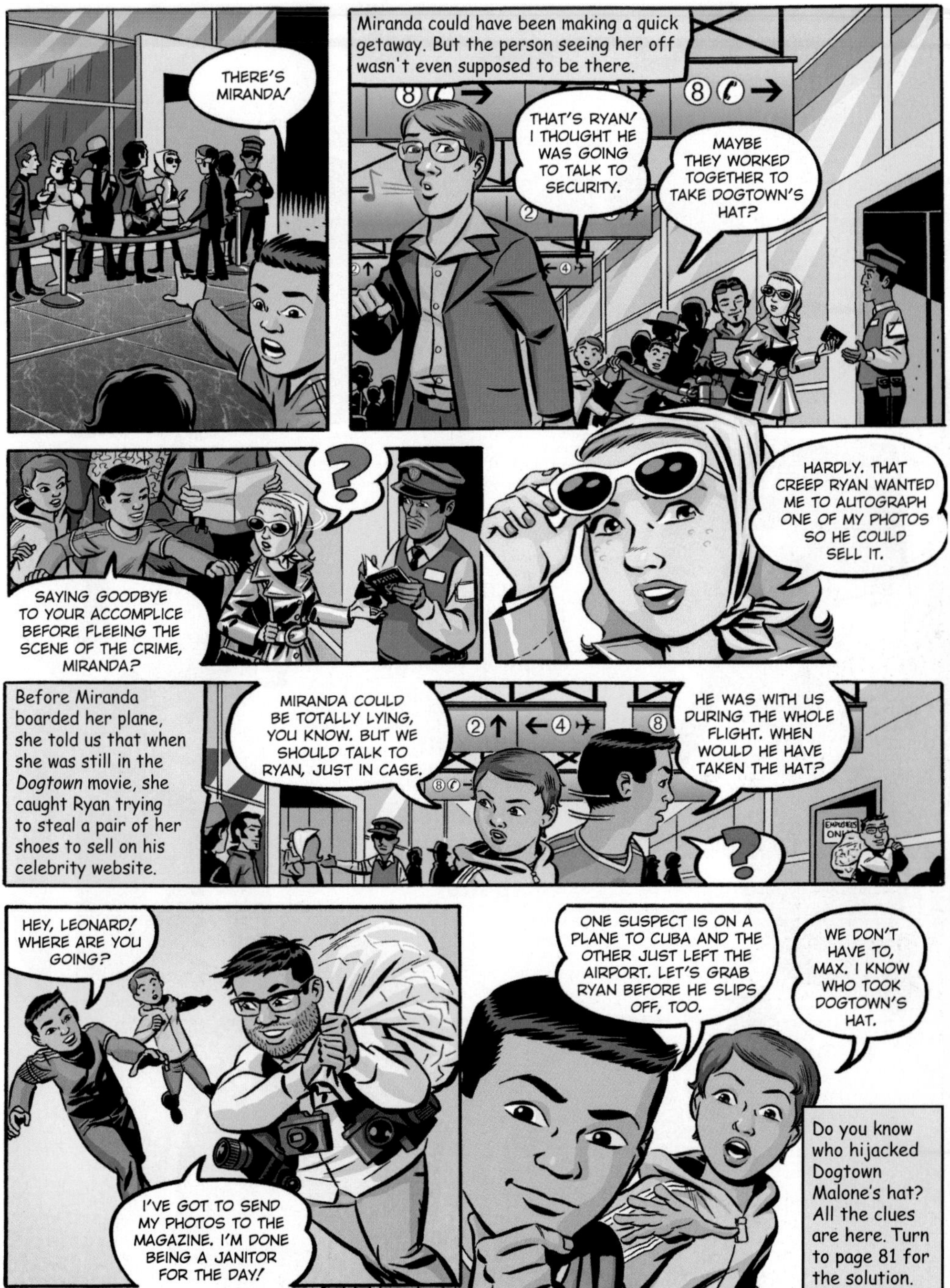
THERE'S MIRANDA!
Miranda could have been making a quick getaway. But the person seeing her off wasn't even supposed to be there.
THAT'S RYAN! I THOUGHT HE WAS GOING TO TALK TO SECURITY.
MAYBE THEY WORKED TOGETHER TO TAKE DOGTOWN'S HAT?
?
SAYING GOODBYE TO YOUR ACCOMPLICE BEFORE FLEEING THE SCENE OF THE CRIME, MIRANDA?
HARDLY. THAT CREEP RYAN WANTED ME TO AUTOGRAPH ONE OF MY PHOTOS SO HE COULD SELL IT.
Before Miranda boarded her plane, she told us that when she was still in the *Dogtown* movie, she caught Ryan trying to steal a pair of her shoes to sell on his celebrity website.
MIRANDA COULD BE TOTALLY LYING, YOU KNOW. BUT WE SHOULD TALK TO RYAN, JUST IN CASE.
HE WAS WITH US DURING THE WHOLE FLIGHT. WHEN WOULD HE HAVE TAKEN THE HAT?
?
HEY, LEONARD! WHERE ARE YOU GOING?
I'VE GOT TO SEND MY PHOTOS TO THE MAGAZINE. I'M DONE BEING A JANITOR FOR THE DAY!
ONE SUSPECT IS ON A PLANE TO CUBA AND THE OTHER JUST LEFT THE AIRPORT. LET'S GRAB RYAN BEFORE HE SLIPS OFF, TOO.
WE DON'T HAVE TO, MAX. I KNOW WHO TOOK DOGTOWN'S HAT.
Do you know who hijacked Dogtown Malone's hat? All the clues are here. Turn to page 81 for the solution.

Chain Reaction

Each photo has something in common with the one beside it.

Can you figure out the connection between the pairs?

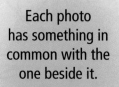

ANSWERS PAGE 85

The Case of the...

Screaming Screening

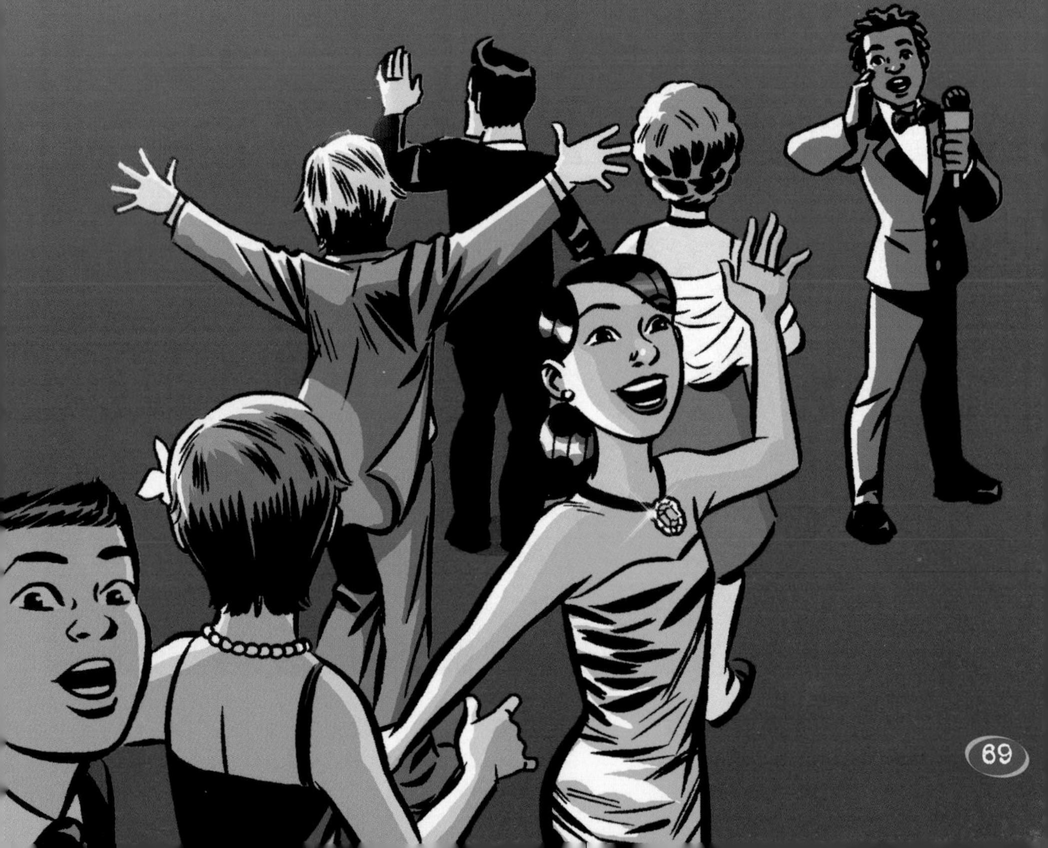

The Case of the Screaming Screening

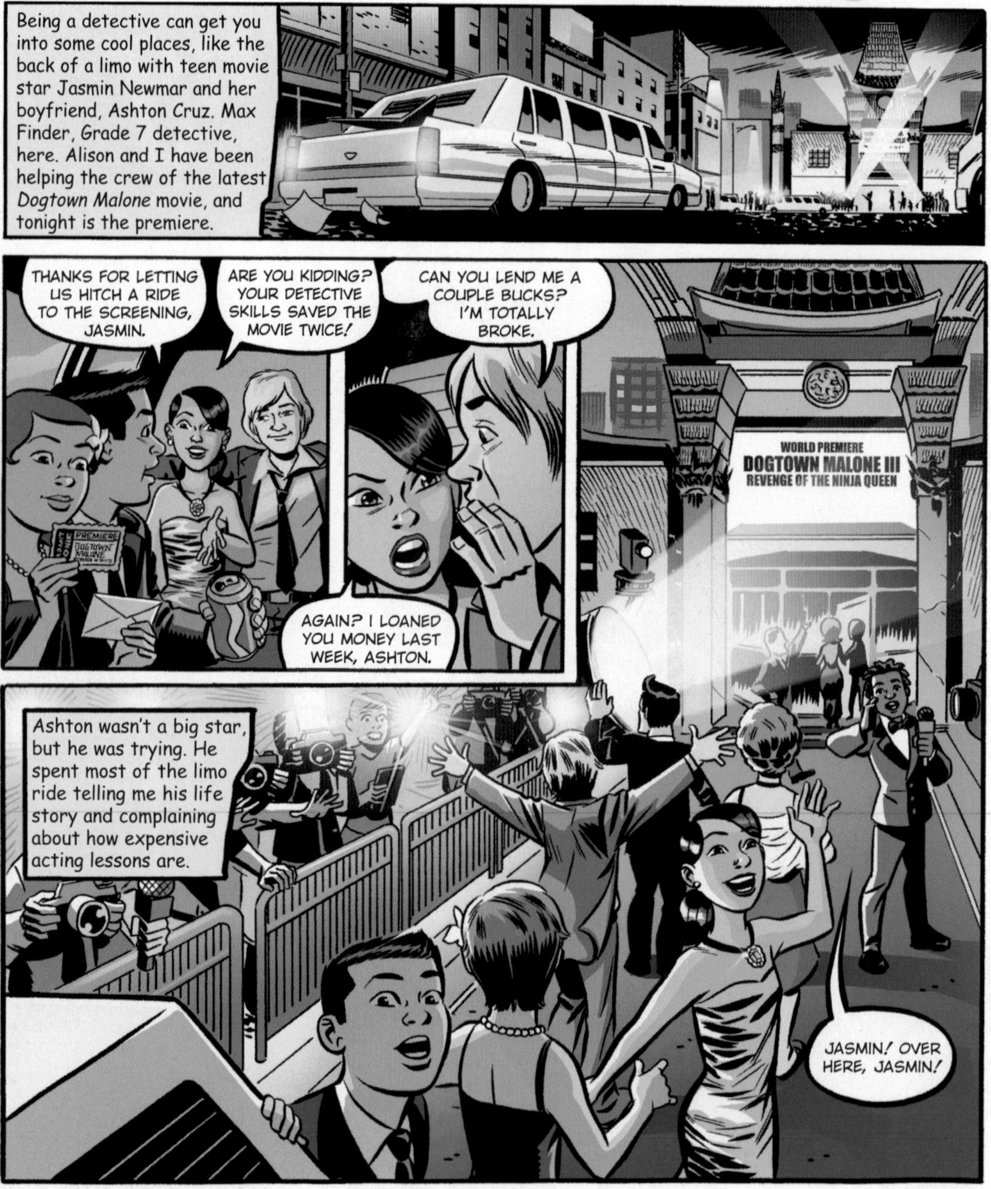
Being a detective can get you into some cool places, like the back of a limo with teen movie star Jasmin Newmar and her boyfriend, Ashton Cruz. Max Finder, Grade 7 detective, here. Alison and I have been helping the crew of the latest *Dogtown Malone* movie, and tonight is the premiere.
THANKS FOR LETTING US HITCH A RIDE TO THE SCREENING, JASMIN.
ARE YOU KIDDING? YOUR DETECTIVE SKILLS SAVED THE MOVIE TWICE!
CAN YOU LEND ME A COUPLE BUCKS? I'M TOTALLY BROKE.
AGAIN? I LOANED YOU MONEY LAST WEEK, ASHTON.
WORLD PREMIERE
DOGTOWN MALONE III
REVENGE OF THE NINJA QUEEN
Ashton wasn't a big star, but he was trying. He spent most of the limo ride telling me his life story and complaining about how expensive acting lessons are.
JASMIN! OVER HERE, JASMIN!

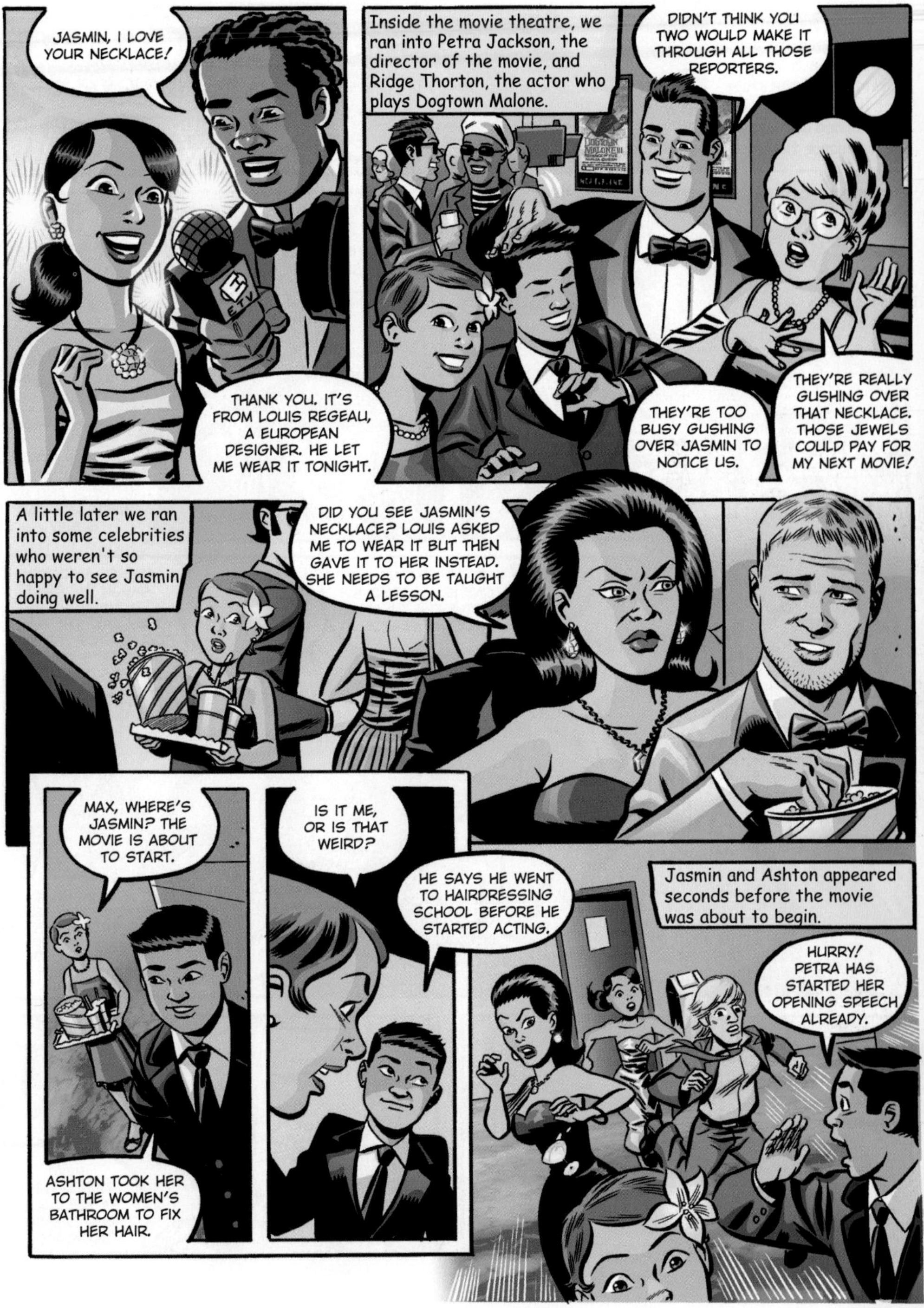
JASMIN, I LOVE YOUR NECKLACE!
THANK YOU. IT'S FROM LOUIS REGEAU, A EUROPEAN DESIGNER. HE LET ME WEAR IT TONIGHT.
Inside the movie theatre, we ran into Petra Jackson, the director of the movie, and Ridge Thorton, the actor who plays Dogtown Malone.
DIDN'T THINK YOU TWO WOULD MAKE IT THROUGH ALL THOSE REPORTERS.
THEY'RE TOO BUSY GUSHING OVER JASMIN TO NOTICE US.
THEY'RE REALLY GUSHING OVER THAT NECKLACE. THOSE JEWELS COULD PAY FOR MY NEXT MOVIE!
A little later we ran into some celebrities who weren't so happy to see Jasmin doing well.
DID YOU SEE JASMIN'S NECKLACE? LOUIS ASKED ME TO WEAR IT BUT THEN GAVE IT TO HER INSTEAD. SHE NEEDS TO BE TAUGHT A LESSON.
MAX, WHERE'S JASMIN? THE MOVIE IS ABOUT TO START.
ASHTON TOOK HER TO THE WOMEN'S BATHROOM TO FIX HER HAIR.
IS IT ME, OR IS THAT WEIRD?
HE SAYS HE WENT TO HAIRDRESSING SCHOOL BEFORE HE STARTED ACTING.
Jasmin and Ashton appeared seconds before the movie was about to begin.
HURRY! PETRA HAS STARTED HER OPENING SPEECH ALREADY.

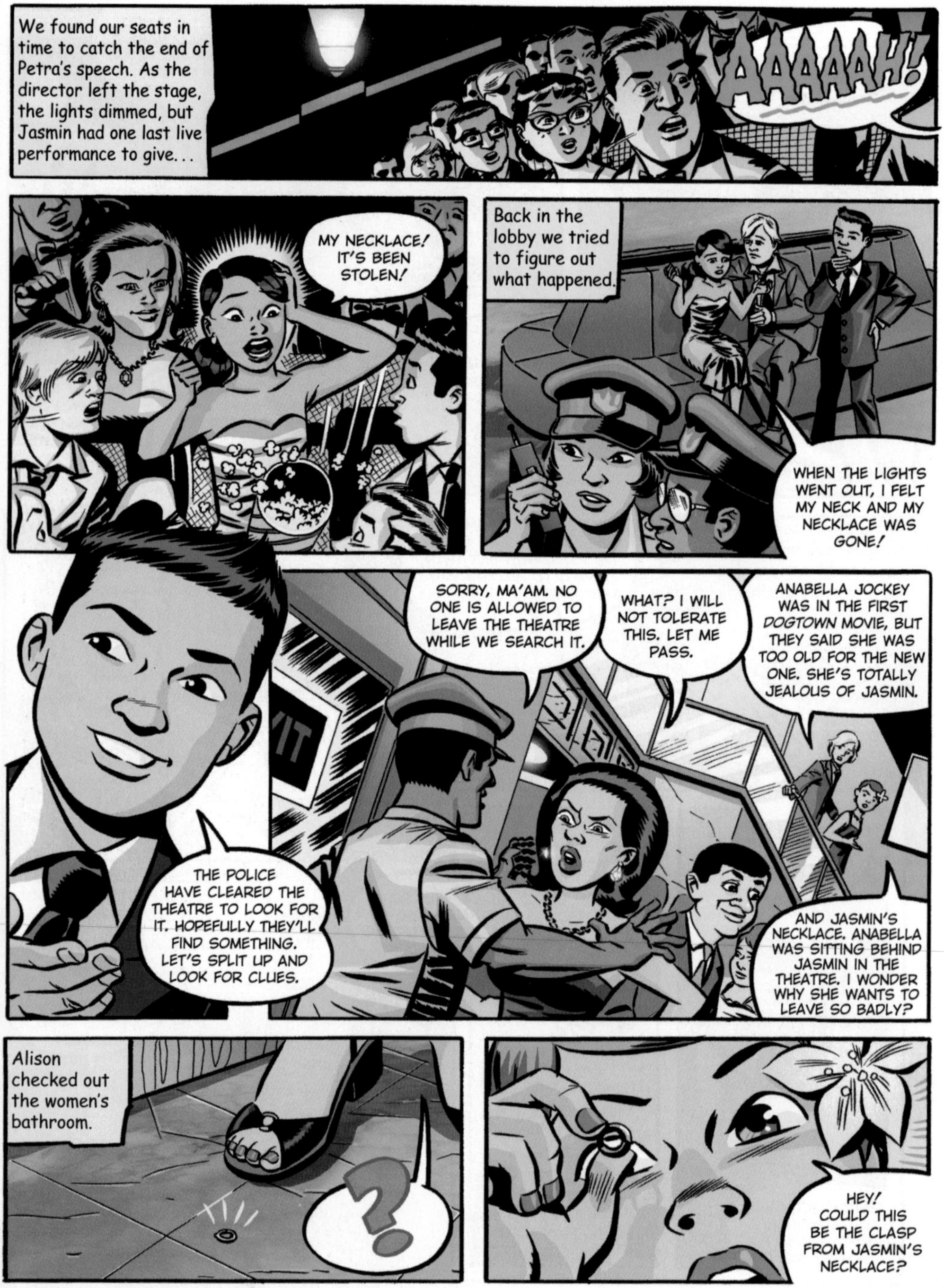

We found our seats in time to catch the end of Petra's speech. As the director left the stage, the lights dimmed, but Jasmin had one last live performance to give...
AAAAAH!
MY NECKLACE! IT'S BEEN STOLEN!
Back in the lobby we tried to figure out what happened.
WHEN THE LIGHTS WENT OUT, I FELT MY NECK AND MY NECKLACE WAS GONE!
SORRY, MA'AM. NO ONE IS ALLOWED TO LEAVE THE THEATRE WHILE WE SEARCH IT.
WHAT? I WILL NOT TOLERATE THIS. LET ME PASS.
ANABELLA JOCKEY WAS IN THE FIRST DOGTOWN MOVIE, BUT THEY SAID SHE WAS TOO OLD FOR THE NEW ONE. SHE'S TOTALLY JEALOUS OF JASMIN.
THE POLICE HAVE CLEARED THE THEATRE TO LOOK FOR IT. HOPEFULLY THEY'LL FIND SOMETHING. LET'S SPLIT UP AND LOOK FOR CLUES.
AND JASMIN'S NECKLACE. ANABELLA WAS SITTING BEHIND JASMIN IN THE THEATRE. I WONDER WHY SHE WANTS TO LEAVE SO BADLY?
Alison checked out the women's bathroom.
?
HEY! COULD THIS BE THE CLASP FROM JASMIN'S NECKLACE?

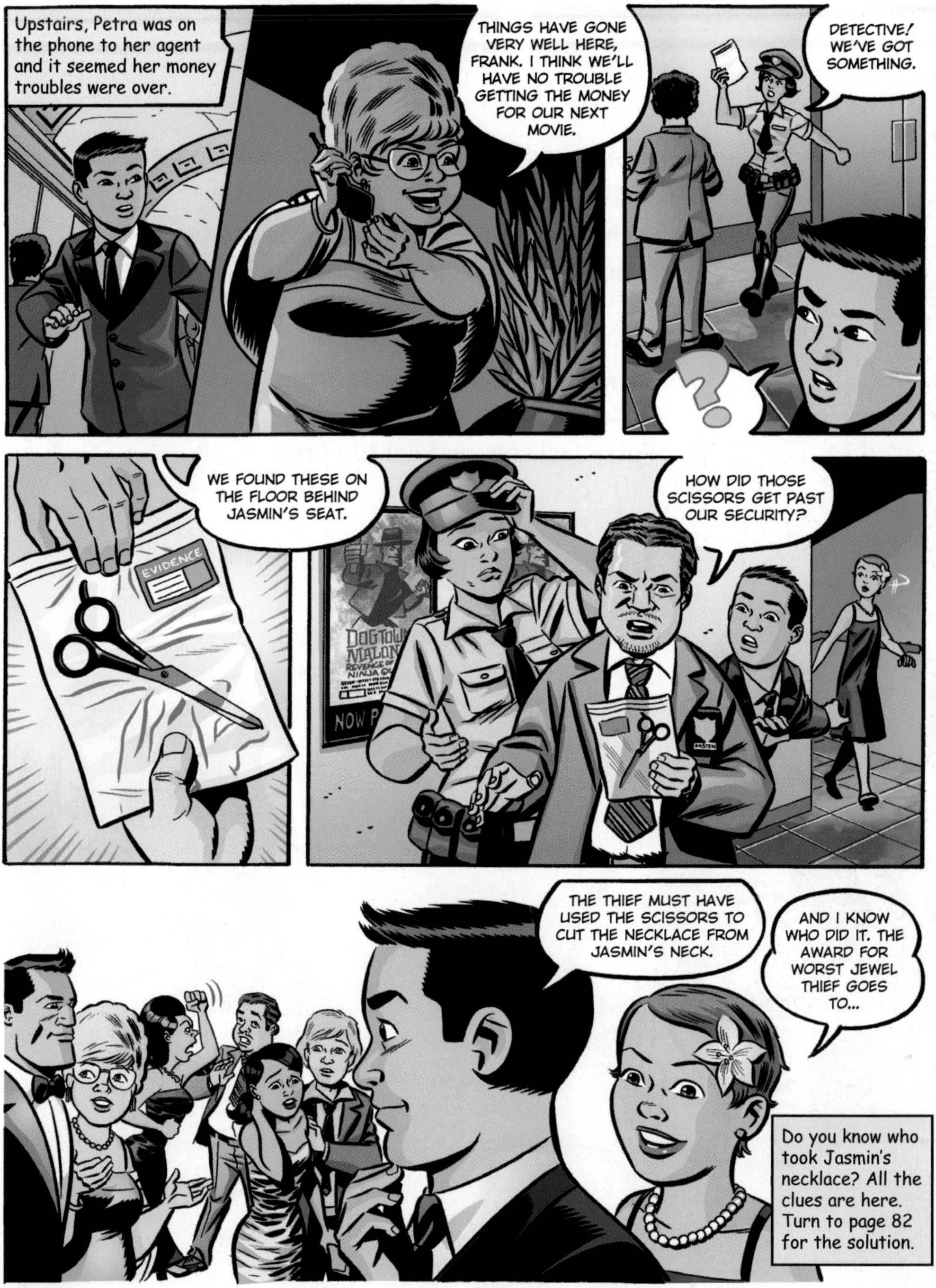
Upstairs, Petra was on the phone to her agent and it seemed her money troubles were over.
THINGS HAVE GONE VERY WELL HERE, FRANK. I THINK WE'LL HAVE NO TROUBLE GETTING THE MONEY FOR OUR NEXT MOVIE.
DETECTIVE! WE'VE GOT SOMETHING.
?
WE FOUND THESE ON THE FLOOR BEHIND JASMIN'S SEAT.
EVIDENCE
HOW DID THOSE SCISSORS GET PAST OUR SECURITY?
NOW P
THE THIEF MUST HAVE USED THE SCISSORS TO CUT THE NECKLACE FROM JASMIN'S NECK.
AND I KNOW WHO DID IT. THE AWARD FOR WORST JEWEL THIEF GOES TO...
Do you know who took Jasmin's necklace? All the clues are here. Turn to page 82 for the solution.

On the Red Carpet

Big-name stars and their bodyguards are walking the red carpet at the screening for Alison's movie.

Look at the clues and work out how many bodyguards each star has.

Hint: **The stars are Jasmin Newmar, Ridge Thorton, Anabella Jockey, Tad Smit, Petra Jackson, and Ashton Cruz.**

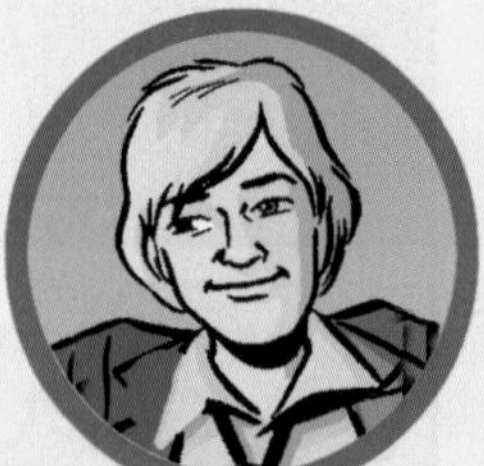

Clues:

1. There are twenty-six bodyguards on the red carpet.

2. One star has just one bodyguard.

3. Anabella has four bodyguards.

4. Tad has twice as many as Petra.

5. Ridge and Jasmin have the same number of bodyguards.

6. Petra has one more bodyguard than Anabella.

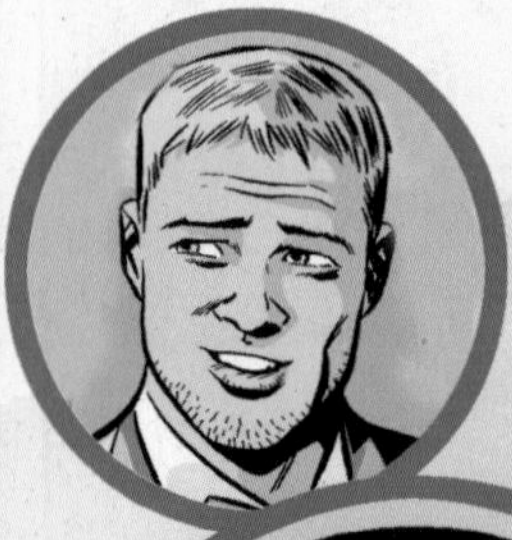

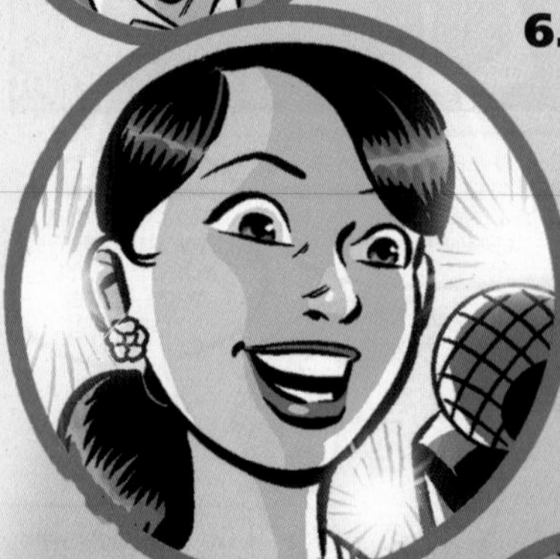

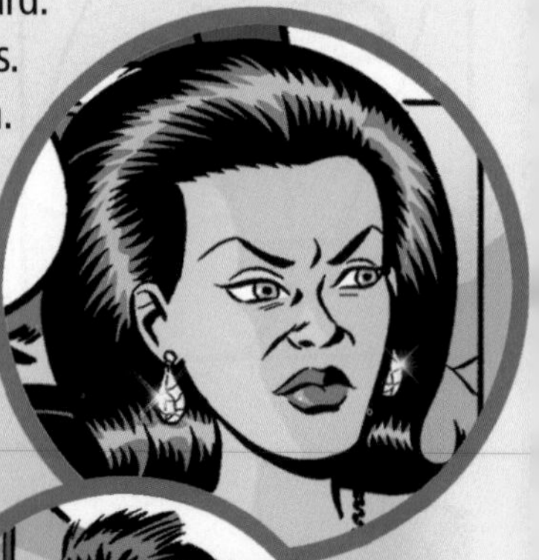

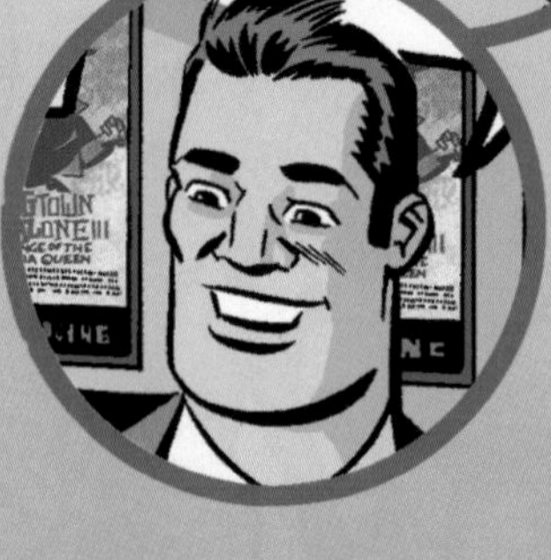

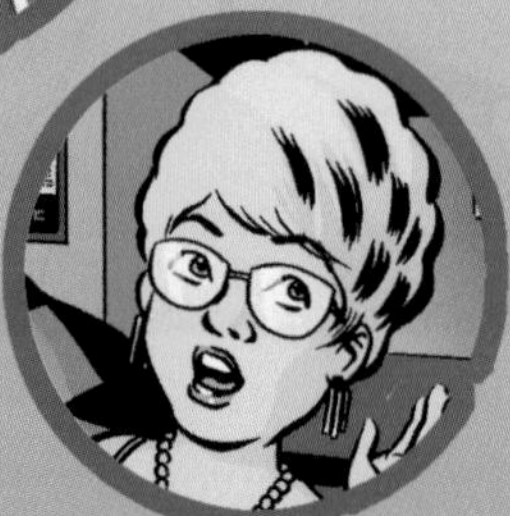

ANSWER PAGE 85

who?
what?
when?
Where?
how?
why?

Case Solutions

The Case of the Back-to-School Sneak
(page 11)

Who is stealing stuff at school?
- **Jake Granger.** Jake wanted everyone to think he was a great detective, so he took things, hid them, and then pretended to find them.

How did Max solve the case?
- Jake worked hard to put the blame on somebody else. But Basher couldn't have been climbing on the garden shed because he was inside serving detention at the time. Jake wore Basher's jacket.
- Jake cut the leather fibres from Basher's jacket. He planted them at Leslie's desk to put suspicion on the bully.
- Taking someone's watch is a classic magic trick. Jake took Leslie's watch when he was doing the "pull a coin from the ear" trick.
- Jake put Leslie's watch in jelly to make it look like one of Kyle's practical jokes. Max overheard Kyle give Jake the idea.

Conclusion
The detectives confronted Jake with the evidence in private. Jake admitted to the thefts and apologized to the class. At first the kids were mad, but after fixing Basher's jacket and doing a few magic tricks, Jake was one of the gang again.

The Case of the Haunted Haunted House
(page 17)

Who or what is haunting Old Oak Manor?
- **Hazel.** She loved the garden so much that she made it look like the house was really haunted to scare Mr. Peeves out of tearing it down.

How did Max solve the case?
- Hazel used old soup cans for plant pots. They were the same cans used to make noise in the house.
- When she scared Max and Alison in the backyard, Hazel had string stuffed into her coat pockets. The same string was used to tie the soup cans together.

Case Solutions

- The rope leading out of the attic window was how Hazel escaped. She had used the rope to sneak behind Max, Alison, and Jessica.
- Basher had already fled the house when Max and Alison heard the eerie voice for the second time. Although he had been sneaking around the house, Basher couldn't have been the haunter.

Conclusion

Hazel was found hiding in the bushes behind the manor and admitted to making the house seem haunted.

With the haunting mystery solved, the actors went to work just as the first party guests arrived. Hazel even used her haunting tools in the attic to make it the best haunted-house party that anyone could remember.

The Case of the Mars Malfunction

(page 23)

Who is sabotaging the space mission?

- **Hans Olo.** Hans was angry at not being picked as captain. First, he tried to get Dorothy in trouble so he could be made captain. When that didn't work, Hans tried to ruin the whole mission.

How did Max solve the case?

- Max and Alison couldn't find the kid who delivered the phony message because he didn't exist. Hans made him up to get Dorothy in trouble.
- Hans had the keys to the Maintenance Room. That meant he could have cut the power to the computers.
- Hans took a yellow vest and an orange hat from the Maintenance Room when he was getting the vest for Drew. He wore them when he stole the Log Book.
- When Hans arrived at the Research Lab, he had his green vest on backwards because he changed so quickly.

Conclusion

Hans admitted to stealing the Log Book. He hid the book in the sludge and dumped the vest and hat in the garbage just before Max and Alison arrived. Commander Ripley pulled Hans off Team Discovery. Both teams landed on Mars, and both missions were declared a success.

Case Solutions

The Case of the Ice Village Vandal

(page 29)

Who stole the elf's circuit board?

- **Mr. Kroft.** The lights from the sign were keeping him up at night, so he snuck into the elf and stole the circuit board.

How did Max and Alison solve the case?

- Max saw Mr. Kroft use keys to sneak into the clubhouse. That reminded Max that Lindsey had said Zack was always losing his keys. When Mr. Kroft cut Zack a new pair of keys, he cut a set for himself so he could sneak into the elf.
- The note Mr. Dumont found demanded that the sign be turned off at night. Only Mr. Kroft was bothered by the lights at night. Everyone else complained about the noise of the moving arm.
- When the note was left in the golf clubhouse, Zack and Becca were in the woods and Lindsey was at home. Only Mr. Kroft was around to plant the note.
- Zack was showing Becca some owl pellets he found in the woods. It proved that the snowy owl was living on the golf course.

Conclusion

Mr. Kroft admitted to stealing the circuit board and returned it to Mr. Dumont. When shown the snowy owl pellets, Mr. Dumont agreed to turn off the statue's moving arm so the birds wouldn't be scared. He also turned off the sign after the Ice Village closed for the night. That way Mr. Kroft could get some sleep.

The Case of the Cast-off Costume

(page 35)

Who smashed the Grouch costume?

- **Basher McGintley.** Although Basher enjoyed being in the holiday pageant, he was embarrassed by his Grouch costume. He thought that if he damaged the costume he would be allowed to wear his jeans on stage.

How did Basher do it?

- After Saturday's rehearsal, Basher wedged Jeff Coleman's henchman hat in the fire exit door. After everyone left, Basher snuck back and took the costume to the tobogganing hill and smashed it.

Case Solutions

How did Max solve the case?

- Courtney mentioned that Basher didn't like the costume. And Mrs. Janssen said Basher had asked to wear his jeans on stage instead.
- Only Basher and Jessica wore red wool hats. But Jessica's mittens and hat were made of expensive angora, so they didn't match the fibres Zoe found on the Grouch's head. That left only Basher's old red wool toque.
- Max and Alison spied Basher trying to get rid of the henchman hat. The bully was surprised when Dwayne and Shayne arrived and had to drop it in the snow.

Conclusion

After seeing that the wool fibres matched his red toque, Basher admitted to smashing the Grouch costume. He said he covered his cold hands with his red hat when he punched the Grouch's papier-mâché head.

Basher was sorry and still wanted to be in the play. Courtney fixed the costume as best as she could and Basher went on stage. He acted like a movie star and the audience gave him a standing ovation.

The Case of the Slime Tank Sabotage

(page 41)

Who sabotaged the slime tank?

- **Johnny Vile.** Johnny was sick of taking apart the *Punk My Bike* set every week. He sabotaged the slime tank so the quiz show would be cancelled.

How did Max solve the case?

- After the accident, Johnny told Mrs. Finder that he had just arrived at the TV station. But Johnny told Max and Alison that he'd been at the TV station working on the set all morning. Plus, the security guard spotted him at the slime tank early in the morning.
- Johnny knew about the bolts being cut, but Max and Alison hadn't told anyone about the bolts yet.
- There were tools, including a hacksaw, lying around the set of *Punk My Bike*. Johnny used them to cut off the bolt tops.
- Basher found the bolt tops beside the tank. He took them but didn't tell anyone.

Conclusion

Johnny admitted to cutting the bolts. Bull O'Wiley agreed not to cancel the quiz show. The footage of the slime tank bursting was shown on TV around the world and made the quiz show an instant hit with viewers.

Case Solutions

The Case of the Lost Lobster
(page 49)

Who stole Twiggy the lobster?

• **Katlyn.** She thought it was cruel to put the lobster on display. She tried to make it look like Twiggy escaped so Lilly wouldn't keep him in the tank anymore. But Katlyn fell off the stool when scooping Twiggy out of the tank and broke the restaurant window. She panicked. She couldn't afford to fix the window, so she asked Patricio to hide Twiggy in the basement of the theatre overnight. Then, Patricio snapped the lock on Judy's shack so they could hide Twiggy inside and put the blame on her.

How did Alison solve the case?

• Alison spotted Katyln's pink bracelet in Twiggy's tank.

• Lilly was afraid Twiggy would bite her, so she probably wouldn't pick him up.

• Katlyn said Lilly was the only person with keys to the restaurant, but Katlyn told Patricio she had to lock up the restaurant.

• When Katlyn arrived for their picnic, Patricio said, "We haven't been waiting long." He had Twiggy in the cooler.

• Alison's uncle's cooler smelled of fish the next day because Patricio had used it to carry Twiggy.

• When they found Twiggy in Judy's shack, the locks on the shack were broken. If Judy had put the lobster there, she wouldn't have broken the lock.

Conclusion

Katlyn admitted to taking the lobster and Patricio confessed to helping her. Katlyn didn't lose her job, but much of her wages went to paying for the broken window. Lilly agreed to donate Twiggy to a nearby ocean research centre, where he now lives free from window-banging tourists.

Case Solutions

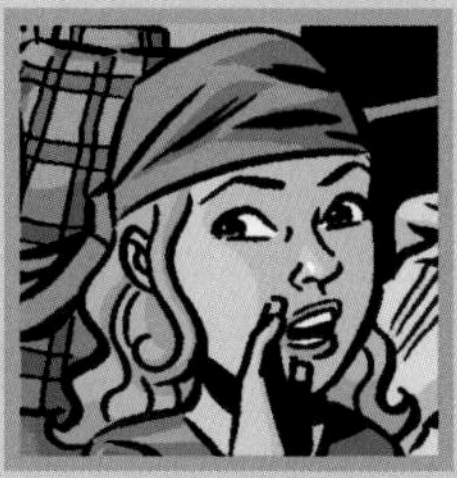

The Case of the Movie Set Mischief

(page 57)

Who is trying to hurt Jasmin?

- **Miranda Madison.** She was mad that she didn't get the role as Dogtown Malone's sidekick. Since they had just started filming the movie, Miranda figured she would get the leading role if Jasmin was hurt.

How did Max solve the case?

- Rex gave Jasmin her lunch, but he got it from Miranda. She had lots of time to put the old tuna into the sandwiches.
- Rex said the ninja who moved the sandbags before the light fell was "skinny." That means it couldn't have been Leonard.
- The ninja who leaped from the bushes was wearing a red bandana — it was Miranda.

Conclusion

Miranda was found hiding out in her hotel room. She admitted she'd tried to hurt Jasmin and was fired from the movie. That night, she slipped out of the hotel and hasn't been seen in the movie business since. Alison eagerly took the job as Jasmin's stunt double.

The Case of the Hijacked Hat

(page 63)

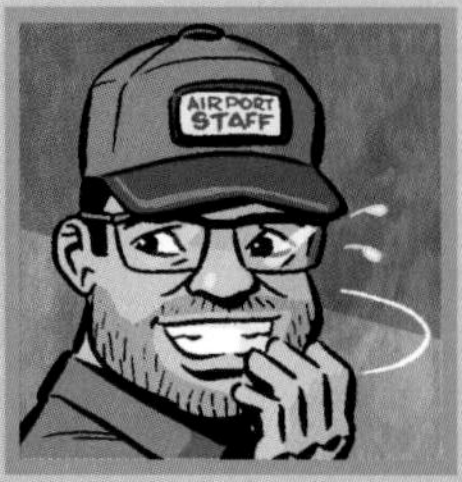
AIRPORT STAFF

Who stole Dogtown Malone's hat?

- **Leonard.** The celebrity photographer was under so much pressure to deliver another scandal for his magazine that he tried to make one by taking Ridge Thorton's lucky hat.

How did Alison solve the case?

- In his janitor's uniform, Leonard had access to the luggage unloading area, where he could take the hat out of the box.
- There was a mysterious brown shape in Leonard's janitor cart.
- When Leonard was leaving the airport he said he was done being a janitor, but he was still carrying a garbage bag. Dogtown's hat was inside the bag.

Conclusion

Airport security caught up with Leonard before he could get away with Dogtown's hat. The celebrity photographer admitted to stealing the hat while the luggage was being unloaded from the plane. Ridge Thorton got his hat back and the movie was finished on time.

Case Solutions

The Case of the Screaming Screening

(page 69)

Conclusion

The police found the necklace in Ashton's pocket and took him away. Everyone returned to their seats to watch *Dogtown Malone III*. It was a huge hit. The audience gave the whole cast, including Max and Alison, a standing ovation.

Who stole Jasmin's necklace?

• **Ashton Cruz.** He needed money to pay for acting lessons, so he snipped off the über-expensive necklace while he was fixing Jasmin's hair in the bathroom.

How did Alison solve the case?

• The scissors found in the balcony were haircutting scissors. Ashton told Max he went to hairdressing school.

• Alison found the necklace clasp in the bathroom, so she knew that's where the robbery took place.

• Jasmin's necklace was missing before she went into the theatre, but she didn't notice until the lights went down.

• Petra was on stage when the jewels were taken, so it couldn't have been her.

• Anabella Jockey was in the lobby while Ashton and Jasmin were in the bathroom, so she couldn't have been the thief.

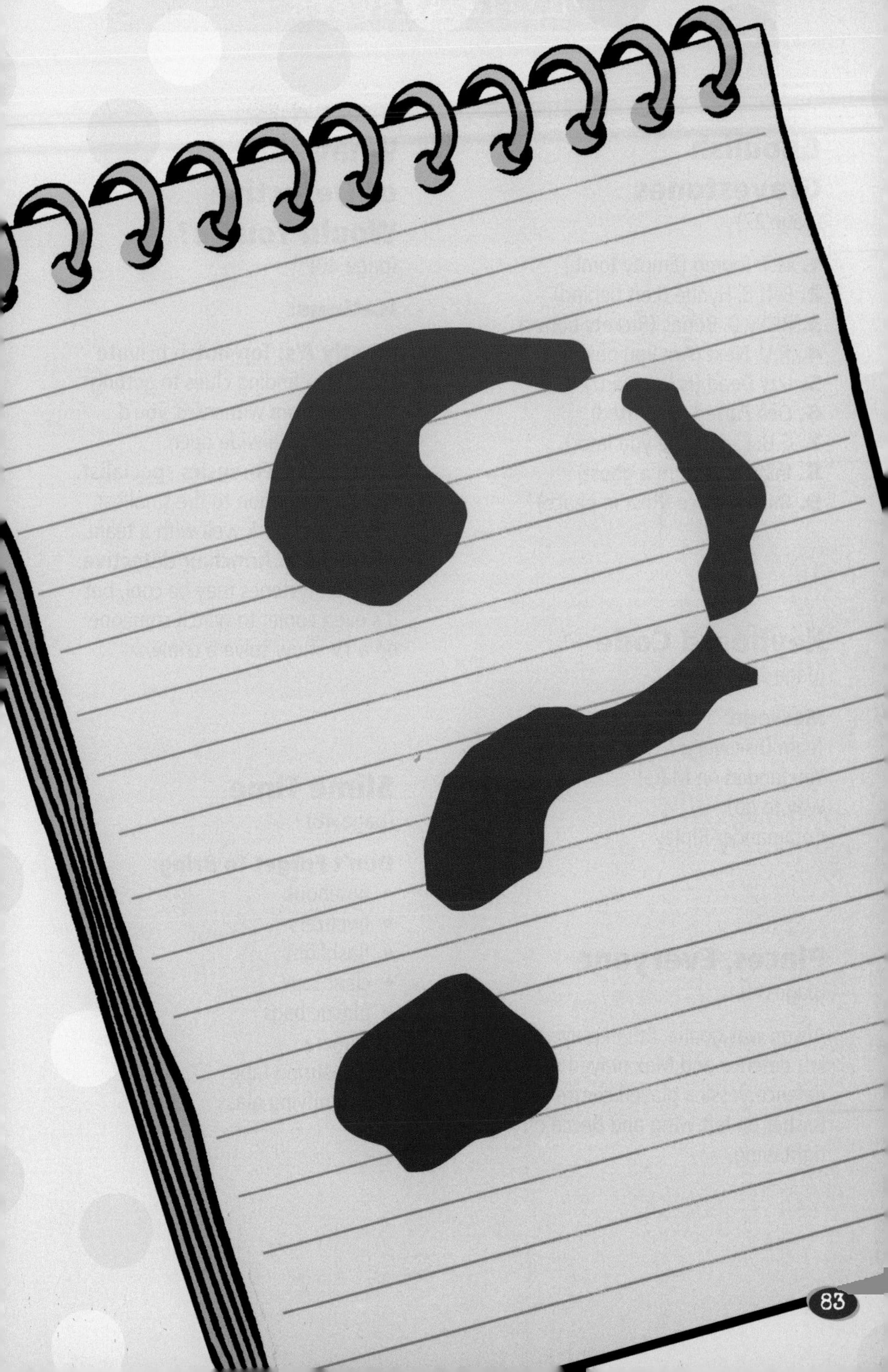

Ghoulish Gravestones
(page 22)

1. M.T. Toomb (Empty tomb)
2. Left B. Hynde (Left behind)
3. Ricky D. Bones (Rickety bones)
4. R.U. Next (Are you next?)
5. Izzy Dead (Is he dead?)
6. Dee Parted (Departed)
7. C.U. Lader (See you later)
8. Ima Ghost (I'm a ghost)
9. Rustin Peace (Rest in peace)

Keyboard Code
(page 28)

Message:
Team Discovery:
You landed on Mars!
Way to go!
Commander Ripley

Places, Everyone
(page 34)

Alison was goalie. Ethan played left defence and Max played right defence. Jessica played centre, with Basher on left wing and Becca on right wing.

What Kind of Detective Would You Be?
(page 40)

Ratings:

Mostly A's: Top-notch private eye. From finding clues to getting the facts from witnesses, you'd crack the case wide open.
Mostly B's: Forensics specialist. You pay attention to the smallest details and work well with a team.
Mostly C's: Armchair detective. Solving mysteries may be cool, but it's even cooler to watch someone on a TV show solve a crime.

Slime Time
(page 48)

Don't Forget to Bring:
- notebook
- tweezers
- flashlight
- clear tape
- plastic bags
- camera
- measuring tape
- magnifying glass

Stick with It
(page 56)

Stamps © Canada Post Corporation (2007). Reproduced with Permission.

1. The three identical stamps are:

2. The stamp that is upside down and backwards is:

3. The stamp from Zimbabwe is:

4. The stamp with a lighthouse on it is:

5. The stamp worth fifteen cents is:

There are **13** Canadian stamps in Max's collection.

Chain Reaction
(page 68)

The common things are:
1. ticket
2. screen
3. keys
4. can be opened
5. arrive by delivery
6. round
7. string
8. fly

Photos (p. 68): travelpixpro/iStockphoto (theatre); Redbaron/ Dreamstime (laptop); xyno/iStockphoto (door); haveseen/iStockphoto (envelope); khz/iStockphoto (pizza); webking/iStockphoto (yo-yo); mashabuba/iStockphoto (kite); Kickers/iStockphoto (plane).

On the Red Carpet
(page 74)

- Tad has **10** bodyguards
- Petra has **5**
- Anabella has **4**
- Ridge and Jasmin have **3**
- Ashton has **1**

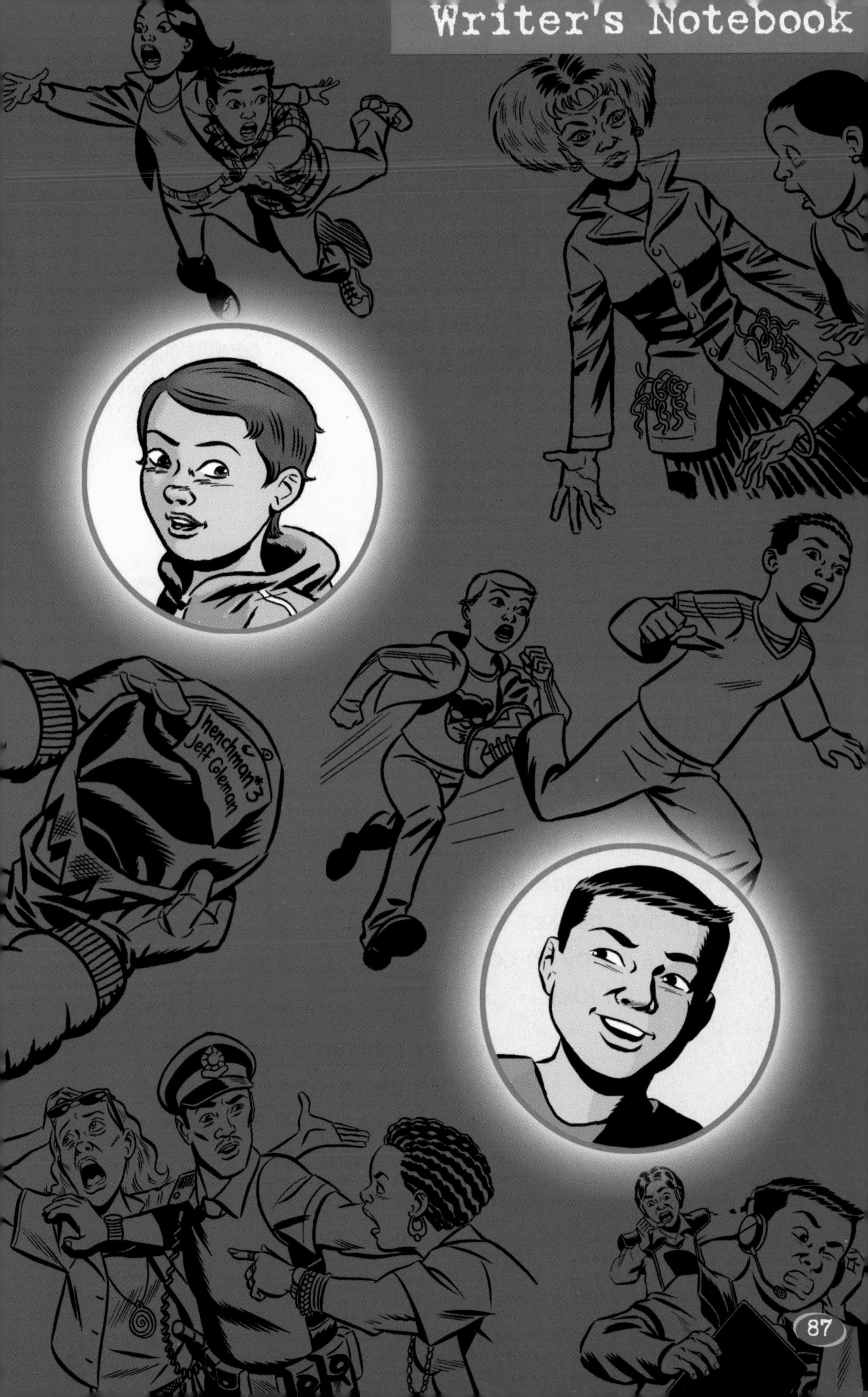
henchman*3
Jeff Gleman

How to Write Your Own Comic

DID YOU KNOW ANYONE CAN WRITE COMICS? LIAM O'DONNELL HERE, *MAX FINDER MYSTERY* CREATOR. FROM SUPERHERO ACTION ADVENTURES TO PUZZLING MYSTERIES, YOU CAN TELL ANY STORY WITH COMICS. AND I'M GOING TO SHOW YOU HOW TO WRITE ONE.

WE BETTER GET OUT OF HERE BEFORE WE'RE CAUGHT.

THAT SOUNDED LIKE DOROTHY! I THINK THE YELL CAME FROM THE LOG ROOM.

SOMEONE STOLE OUR MISSION LOG BOOK!

SOMEONE ANGE CAP THE HALL!

Catching Ideas

Every comic starts with an idea, and it can land in your brain at any time. I carry a notebook that fits my jacket pocket so I'm always ready to catch an idea.

Sometimes a writer's brain is empty of ideas. When this happens, I ask myself: "What if...?" Then I put something that doesn't happen every day after the "if" to give me a story idea.

ROP THAT AMES!

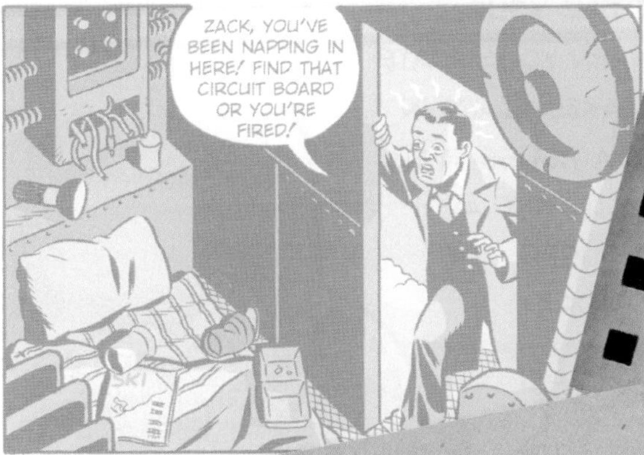
ZACK, YOU'VE BEEN NAPPING IN HERE! FIND THAT CIRCUIT BOARD OR YOU'RE FIRED!

Max Finder Mystery Ideas

What if...

- Basher hired Max to solve a crime?

- Max and Alison solved a mystery at the zoo — an escaped koala?

- Alison was accused of a crime and Max had to prove she was innocent?

THE SETTING IS THE PLACE AND TIME YOUR STORY HAPPENS. BE SPECIFIC WHEN YOU CREATE YOUR SETTING. IF YOUR STORY TAKES PLACE IN A HOUSE, DESCRIBE THE HOUSE. A HOUSE IN THE CITY, A SPOOKY MANSION ON A HILL, AND A COTTAGE BY THE SEA ARE ALL HOUSES, BUT EACH COULD TELL A DIFFERENT STORY.

WE BETTER GET OUT OF HERE BEFORE WE'RE CAUGHT.

BEING SPECIFIC NOT ONLY CREATES A BETTER STORY FOR YOUR READERS, IT ALSO TELLS YOUR ILLUSTRATOR WHAT TO DRAW. BUT DON'T HOG ALL THE CREATIVITY! LET THE ILLUSTRATOR ADD HIS OR HER IDEAS AND YOU'LL HAVE AN EVEN BETTER COMIC.

MAKE YOUR CHARACTERS UNIQUE BY AVOIDING STEREOTYPES, THOSE OVERLY SIMPLE CHARACTERS YOU'VE SEEN BEFORE. THE PIMPLY-FACED COMPUTER NERD WHO GETS BULLIED IS AN EXAMPLE OF A STEREOTYPE. A GOOD WAY TO AVOID STEREOTYPES IS TO GIVE YOUR CHARACTERS AN UNEXPECTED INTEREST THAT DOESN'T FIT THE STEREOTYPE. BASHER MCGINTLEY IS A GROUCHY BULLY, BUT HE ALSO LOVES ACTING IN SCHOOL PLAYS.

WRITERS CREATE CHARACTER SKETCHES FOR ILLUSTRATORS TO USE WHEN THEY'RE DRAWING. IN A FEW SENTENCES, DESCRIBE WHAT YOUR CHARACTERS LOOK LIKE, HOW OLD THEY ARE, WHAT THEY LIKE WEARING, AND ANYTHING ELSE THAT MAKES THEM UNIQUE. HERE'S A CHARACTER SKETCH OF JAKE GRANGER.

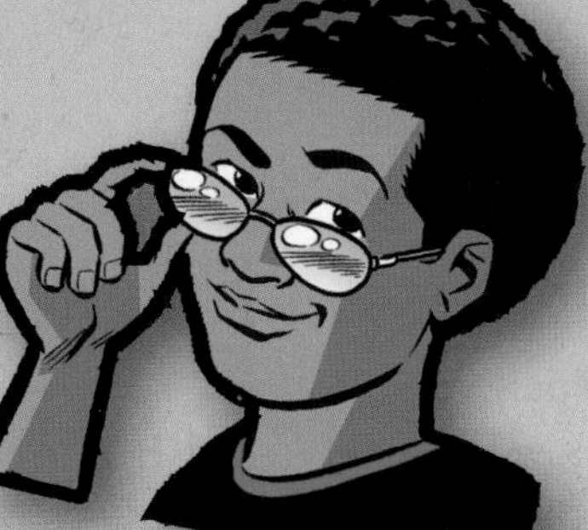

Jake Granger – Tall, 12-year-old African-Canadian with action-hero good looks. He likes magic and thinks he is psychic. He also plays sports and loves being outside. He wears skater-style clothes – semi-baggy jeans, cool T-shirts, and chunky skater shoes.

Building the Plot

YOUR CHARACTERS NEED SOMETHING TO DO, SO IT'S TIME TO CREATE YOUR PLOT. THE BEST PLOTS INVOLVE A PROBLEM YOUR CHARACTER MUST SOLVE. THINK OF YOUR CHARACTERS AS RIDING A BIKE UP A HILL. USE YOUR IMAGINATION AND FOLLOW THESE STEPS:

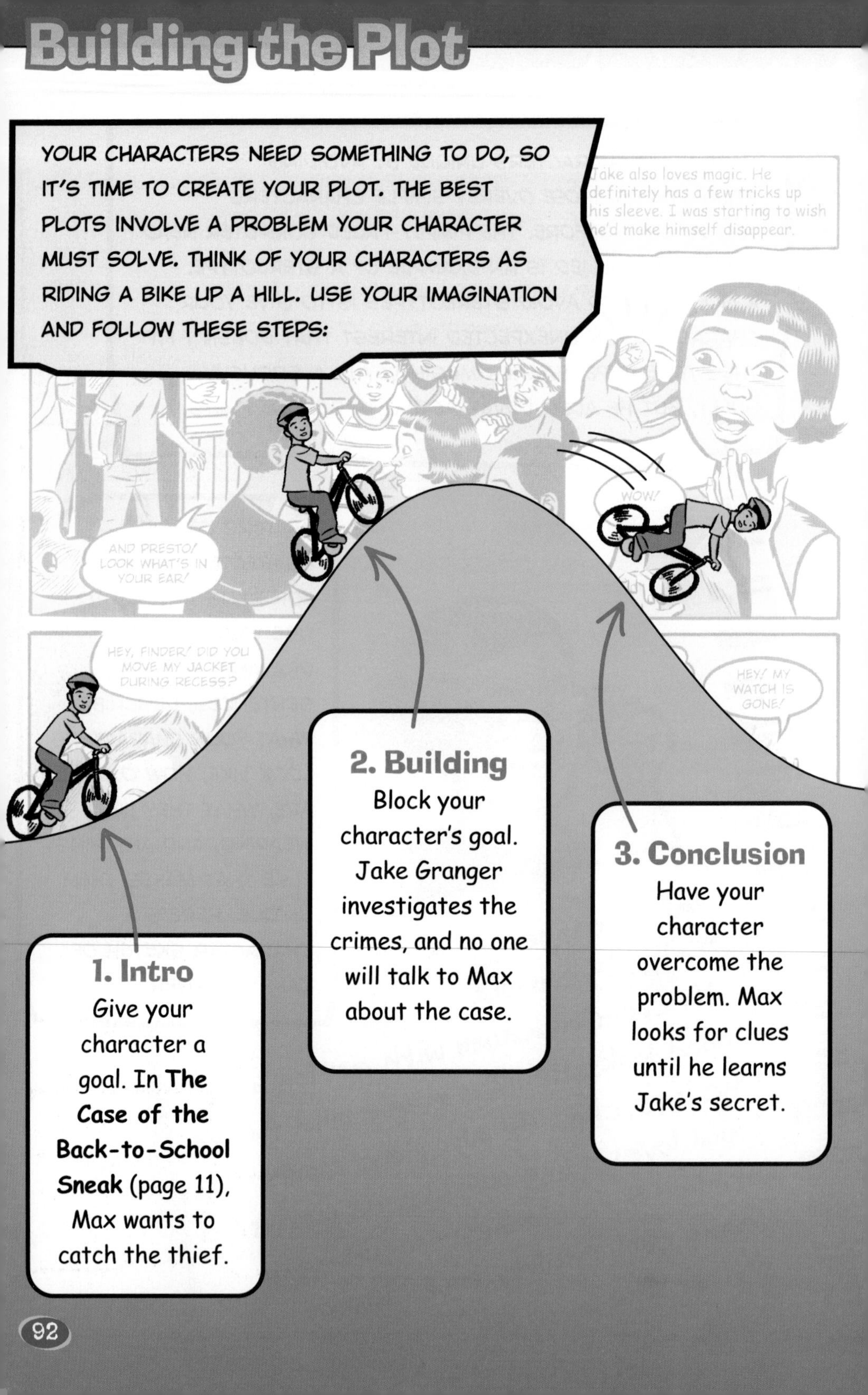
Jake also loves magic. He definitely has a few tricks up his sleeve. I was starting to wish he'd make himself disappear.
AND PRESTO! LOOK WHAT'S IN YOUR EAR!
WOW!
HEY, FINDER! DID YOU MOVE MY JACKET DURING RECESS?
HEY! MY WATCH IS GONE!

1. Intro
Give your character a goal. In **The Case of the Back-to-School Sneak** (page 11), Max wants to catch the thief.

2. Building
Block your character's goal. Jake Granger investigates the crimes, and no one will talk to Max about the case.

3. Conclusion
Have your character overcome the problem. Max looks for clues until he learns Jake's secret.

Writing the Script

NOW YOU'RE READY TO START WRITING YOUR COMIC SCRIPT. A COMIC SCRIPT IS PART STORY AND PART ILLUSTRATION MANUAL TELLING THE ILLUSTRATOR WHAT TO DRAW. HERE'S WHAT A MAX FINDER MYSTERY SCRIPT LOOKS LIKE:

Put the author's name, comic title, draft number, and date at the top of every page.

Comic page number shows which comic page you're working on.

The **scene description** tells the illustrator what to draw.

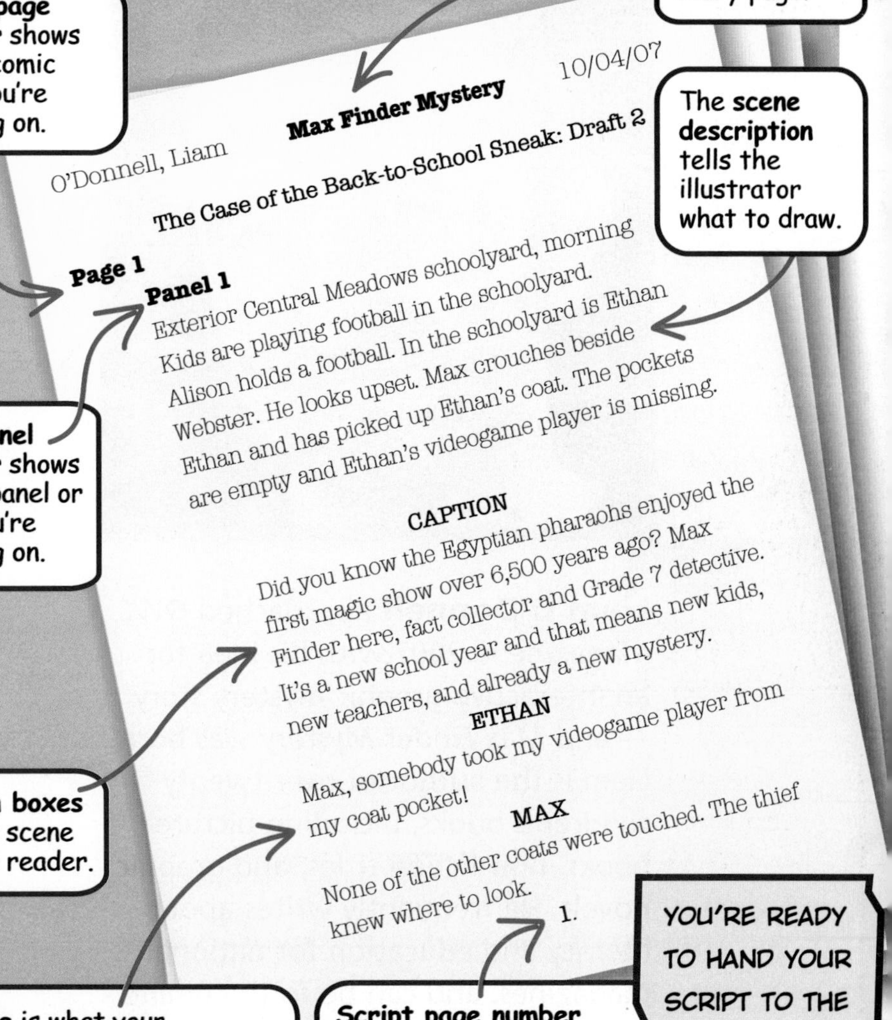
O'Donnell, Liam **Max Finder Mystery** 10/04/07

The Case of the Back-to-School Sneak: Draft 2

Page 1

Panel 1

Exterior Central Meadows schoolyard, morning

Kids are playing football in the schoolyard. Alison holds a football. In the schoolyard is Ethan Webster. He looks upset. Max crouches beside Ethan and has picked up Ethan's coat. The pockets are empty and Ethan's videogame player is missing.

CAPTION

Did you know the Egyptian pharaohs enjoyed the first magic show over 6,500 years ago? Max Finder here, fact collector and Grade 7 detective. It's a new school year and that means new kids, new teachers, and already a new mystery.

ETHAN

Max, somebody took my videogame player from my coat pocket!

MAX

None of the other coats were touched. The thief knew where to look.

1.

The panel number shows which panel or box you're working on.

Caption boxes set the scene for the reader.

Dialogue is what your characters say. Add the character's name to show who is talking. Keep dialogue short to fit the speech bubble.

Script page number refers to the pages in your comic script. There are usually more script pages than comic pages.

YOU'RE READY TO HAND YOUR SCRIPT TO THE ILLUSTRATOR.

Liam O'Donnell

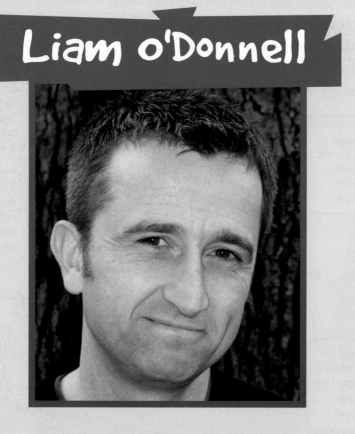

Liam O'Donnell approached *OWL Magazine* in 2002 with his idea for an interactive graphic mystery story — and *Max Finder Mystery* was born. Liam is the author of over twenty children's books, including picture books, non-fiction titles, and graphic novels. He frequently writes about literacy and education for national magazines, and can be found online at www.liamodonnell.com.

Michael Cho

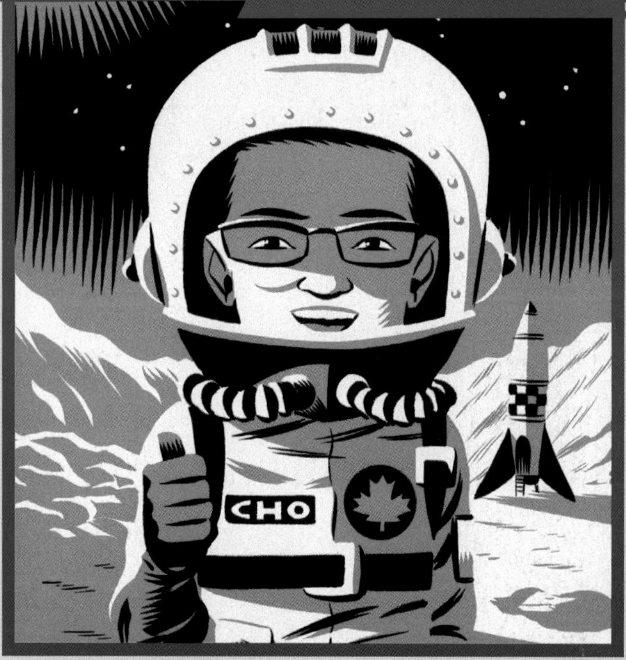
CHO

Michael Cho was born in Seoul, South Korea, and moved to Canada when he was six years old. A graduate of the Ontario College of Art and Design, Michael has published his distinctive drawings and comics in magazines across North America and has illustrated several children's books, including *Media Madness: An Insider's Guide to Media*. He is currently devoting his time to writing and drawing more comics, and you can always see his latest work online at www.michaelcho.com.

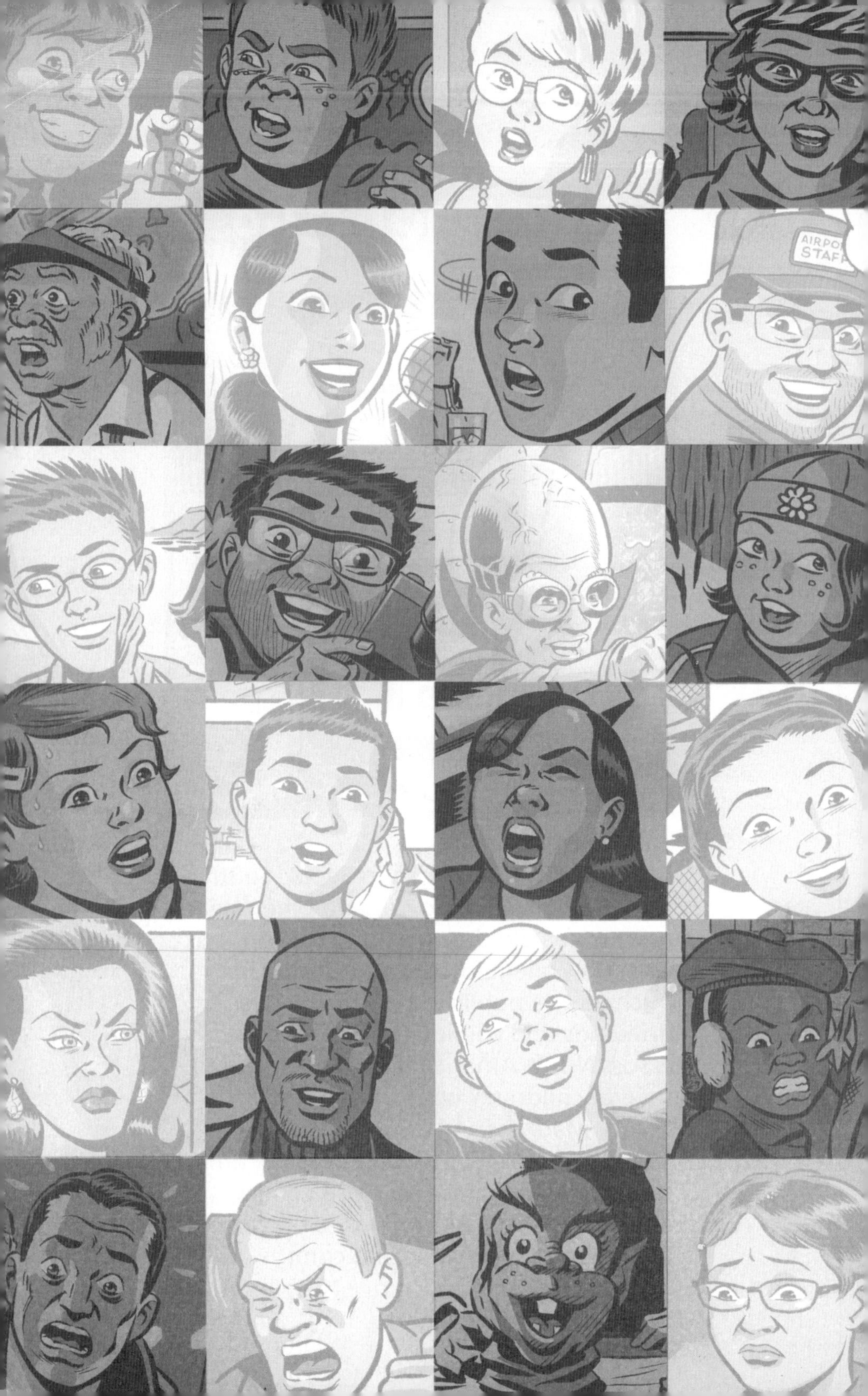
AIRPO
STAFF